The Slave Girl

A Novel

The Slave Girl
Buchi Emecheta

George Braziller
New York

First published by George Braziller, Inc., in the United
States of America in 1977

Originally published in Great Britain by Allison & Busby
Limited

For information, please address the publisher:
George Braziller, Inc.
171 Madison Avenue
New York, NY 10016

Library of Congress Cataloging-in-Publication Data:
Emecheta, Buchi.
    The slave girl.
    I. Title.
PZ4.E525S1 1980 [PR9387.9.E387] 823 79-25651
ISBN 0-8076-0952-8

Printed and bound in the United States of America

Eleventh paperback printing, 2008

To Margaret Busby
for her believing in me

Contents

The Slave Girl

Prologue

The Eke Market was the centre of all that mattered in Ibuza. It was one of the biggest markets in the whole mid-western region, and so famous was it that traders came from all the neighbouring towns to buy and sell. It was not quite certain why that particular spot was chosen for the big market. It was not there that the founder of Ibuza, a young prince called Umejei, had first landed; he had landed at a village called Omeze. The prince had come from Isu, an Ibo town in the eastern part of Nigeria, but he had been sent into exile for accidentally killing his opponent in what started as a friendly wrestling match. To the people of Isu it was always a case of a life for a life; it did not matter whether one of the lives was that of a pedlar and the other that of a beloved prince like the gallant Umejei. However, his life was spared on the condition that he left Isu.

His father, the Oba of Isu, brokenhearted, sent Umejei away with blessings and a gourd of medicine to guard him. He told his son: "Where this gourd drops to the ground, there shall be your home, and there you shall increase and multiply, and your people, your sons and daughters, shall fill the new town, and that town will grow and will always be yours. I forgive you for what happened; it was a misfortune. But in our clan all souls are equal, none is greater than the other. The law of our land will not permit you to stay in Isu and live, so you must go, and go in peace."

When Umejei left Isu, his mother, one of the king's chief wives, decided to go with him, for she said to herself, "What am I without the comfort of my only son?" His sisters followed him as well. So it was a small group of pioneers that set out that day to make their way through the thick tropical jungle of what was then Western Nigeria. They must have crossed the Niger — a big river, too wide and dangerous to be waded through. When they reached the spot now known as Omeze, Umejei had a fall, and the town of Ibuza was founded.

9

He could not have chosen a better place to found a new town. The river Oboshi washed the area on one side, a very deep, clear river with so many fish that in those days Umejei could almost catch them with his bare hands. From the other side ran the Atakpo stream which was also extremely useful to those early farmers; it was quite shallow, falling through many rocks, and it was a beauty to watch. It had clear sands in which grew a myriad African tropical plants with broad leaves that looked as if they had been washed clean by some delicate invisible hand.

(Now before you reach Ibuza, after leaving the River Niger near Onitsha you walk towards the busy market town of Asaba and then go straight ahead for only a few miles, a few hours' trek. On the way you have to pass walls of thick forest, and many farms, before you come to the Atakpo stream, in a valley, and it is then that its beauty will strike you.)

Facing was a steeply sloping hill which carried thick vegetation and gave the impression that beyond this place no human dared ever live. However it was inside this dense natural protection that the prince Umejei and those early pioneers established their settlement. (Now there is a road there, still struggling to asserts its existence against nature, for everything grows in abundance in an area like this.) Apart from being surrounded by rich vegetation and water in plenty, Ibuza was surrounded by neighbours — some friendly, some not so friendly, although after hundreds of years of living close together they were all to learn to respect each other. The name Ibuza, which meant "Ibos living in the middle of the road", was no doubt given to the town by her neighbours who were already there before Umejei came. The people of Ibuza loved fighting better than food, and they had many successes in the forest battles of those times. It was therefore perhaps not unexpected that while some of the early settlements such as Ogboli still remained villages, Ibuza sprang into a town teeming with people; in fact Ogboli later became the tenth village amalgamated into Ibuza.

When you walked down the main path (which by today's standards is wide enough to take two cars side by side) from the Atakpo stream, you came into an open square on which all the tiny bush tracks converged. Both sides of this major road — which may have been purpose-built or may have been the inevitable result of the trekking of thousands who lived, loved, sorrowed and died in the town — were used as part of the market, which culminated in the central square in the Eke Market.

Hundreds of homesteads were strung out in clusters along bush paths leading from the square, each cluster representing the children and ancestors of a son or relative of the founder of the town. There were nine such clusters, each one big enough to be called a village in its own right. So the people referred to Ibuza as the town of nine slices and, just as the segments of an orange are encased within a firm peel, the segments of Ibuza were held together by their relationship to their forebear, Umejei.

One of the slices of this town was the village of Umuisagba. It was through the cluster of homesteads belonging to the people of Umuisagba that the market ran. These people were always claiming to be in the know — after all, they were the children conceived and given birth to right there in the centre of the town. Did they not see the latest fashions coming from Onitsha, from Asaba, from all the towns in the nearby surroundings, before anyone else? It gave a great sense of pride to be able to tell another Ibuza person, "I come from Umuisagba." This Umuisagba pride was so well known that some conservative homes were reluctant to marry girls from there. "They tend to boast a great deal and are given to much talking. They never forget that they came from the centre, and they never let you forget either. When they drop something or knock their toe against a root, they never call the gods of their husbands' houses to help them — they would rather call upon the goddess of the market to help them out. So if you do not wish your hut to be brought to shame by some woman who would forever be saying, 'Eke help me, Eke save me,' steer clear of the girls from Umuisagba." The latter accusation was very serious indeed. If a good wife was in trouble of any kind, instead of calling on God to help her she could call out either the name of her husband or of the god of her husband's people; certainly not the gods in the huts of her own father, for they should cease to exist for her, the day her bride price is paid. From that day she should be loyal to her husband, his gods and his people, in body and in spirit. The daughters of Umuisagba, however, would never deign to comply with this tradition.

Now during the time of this story, in the early years of the twentieth century, lived Okwuekwu with his wife Umeadi and their two sons.

1 The Slave Girl

An early morning cock crowed, its voice sounding rather strange and distant. The harmonious calls of other birds followed; and all the village was alive with the animal noises of a waking African tropical forest.

"Sons, my sons, it is time for us to go to the farm. Okolie, Owezim — wake up! It is morning."

The young men reluctantly rose from their sleeping mats and greeted their father. Owezim was the bigger boy; at nineteen he stood very tall and straight, and was a promising farmer. He never talked much; it seemed that all his verbal energy was in his head. He thought a great deal, and this gave an illusion of added strength, for people tended to wonder to themselves: "How do we know what other inner power he has hidden there inside him?"

Okolie, on the other hand, was everything his elder brother was not. True, he too was tall, for their parents were a tall couple. But Okolie was noisy, he was not very industrious, and he hated going to the farm. He loved music and would blow at his horn pipe for days on end. For his sixteen years, he was very popular in the village.

"Before we go, Okolie, you will fill my pipe for me. Your mother is not up to it this morning," Okwuekwu said in a low voice to his younger son, who he knew expected his mother to come from her sleeping-mat in the inner room to fill the pipe for her husband.

"But, Father . . ."

"There are no buts about it. It should be your job in the first place. Your mother simply took it on herself to do it. So get up, young man, and fill your father's pipe."

Okolie did not mistake the harsh note in his father's voice that meant suppressed anger which, if not checked, could explode into a terrible outburst. He quickly set about doing as he was told.

It was Owezim who asked, "But what is the matter with Mother

13

this morning? She usually wakes before the cock crows."

"She is tired, son, and her time is very near," Okwuekwu replied meditatively, praying inwardly to Oboshi, the river goddess of their town Ibuza, to help his wife this time. He would have liked a baby girl; but what was the use, when all the girls his wife bore him always died after a few hours.

What was he going to do? They had lost so many children at birth, so many that he could not remember the number. He remembered though that their first child had been a girl who died within hours. Then they had a boy, who lived and grew strong, and he named him Owezim, meaning "I am no longer bitter at my lot". They had had a set of girl twins next, and both died. There were one or two more babies that died before Okolie arrived — "born on the Olie market day". It was an important day for them, a day his wife Umeadi usually went to Asaba to sell her farm products. After Okolie, she had had so many pregnancies that her husband ceased paying much attention to them. However, as they grew older, a thought began to nag at him that perhaps he had better settle for just two sons. Although he was entitled to marry as many wives as he wanted, and he knew many husbands who enjoyed the benefits of polygamy, he was simply not that type of man. It had taken him long enough to get used to Umeadi. Of course a new younger wife would mean another pair of hands on his farm, but he had other employment apart from farming. He was a "Kortu-ma" — a court messenger.

He had been lucky to get this job. An English District Officer had been sent to the troublesome town of Ibuza, where in the year 1900 the elders resisted the white administrators. Other officers were dispatched there in 1909, and they were sent packing not only by the elders but also by their notorious malaria mosquitoes, and many other such tropical insect soldiers. It happened that one District Officer who survived was so ill he could hardly walk, and all his guides had fled in the face of Ibuza determination — it was not for nothing that these people were nicknamed "those Ibos who would rather fight than eat". Somebody, Okwuekwu did not know who, recommended him to the ailing Englishman saying there was an Ibuza man who was very tall, whose heels seldom touched the ground, yet whom you could hear coming even when he was still a long way away. This man had the energy of seven, it was said, and could carry the Englishman safely in his "amoku" through Ibuza to Ogwashi-Ukwu, where the D.O.'s headquarters were. The sick D.O.

14

begged his informant to get him such a man.

Okwuekwu did not have much sympathy for all those pale-skin people; to him there was no difference between any of them. In fact the people of Ibuza — at a time when it was glorious to be an Englishman, when the reign of the great Queen Victoria's son was coming to its close, when the red of the British Empire covered almost half the map of the world, when colonisation was at its height, and Nigeria was being taken over by Great Britain — did not know that they were not still being ruled by the Portuguese. The people of Ibuza did not realise that their country, to the last village, was being amalgamated and partitioned by the British. They knew nothing of what was happening; they did not know that there were other ways of robbing people of their birthright than by war. The African of those days was very trusting.

However, humanity prevailed: Okwuekwu, despite opposition from his people, carried the weak English administrator in his hammock to Ogwashi-Ukwu. When others challenged him, asking why he should carry a white man who wanted to stay in their town only to fight them, Okwuekwu replied: "But is it not a wicked man who would fight someone who is knocking at the gates of death?" In this prognosis Okwuekwu was to be proved wrong; although the white men looked fragile, they were cunning and could be extremely strong. That white man lived to tell his story; and as a result when a new District Officer was appointed he sought out Okwuckwu and gave him the lucrative job of "Kortu-ma", in remembrance of his past services.

It was now over a year since he had rescued the dying English-man. In this job as court messenger he followed the translation of the court proceedings by a slave interpreter from Akwa. Okwuekwu himself could neither speak nor understand English or Portuguese, let alone tell the difference between them, but he could tell when the European D.O. wanted some peace and quiet to listen to a case. Things in the Ibuza native court often turned into a verbal contest which became so heated that you could not hear your own voice. And this was when Okwuekwu was needed. He would put his hands behind his back, take a few menacing steps as if to bear down on the offender, and then shout, "Oda!" The newly installed D.O. had many times tried to teach him to repeat the whole sentence — "Order in the court", or "Silence in this court" — but Okwuekwu could not be bothered with all that, and continued to use his own version. What was the point of learning a lot of meaningless sounds

15

when one word would do? He had asked the new D.O. this question through the interpreter and the interpreter had told the D.O. that Okwuekwu said he would say "Oda!" and no more. The Englishman had laughed to himself, remembering the warning he had been given about these Ibo people on the west of the Niger; he had said, "Have it your own way, chief."

Okwuekwu had smiled, and he had chewed kolanut with the new D.O. and his interpreter (who was called locally the "tapilita"). He had got the job and the name Okwuekwu Oda had stuck.

So if you came to Umuisagba, one of the nine villages that made up the town of Ibuza, searching for a man called Okwuekwu, people would ask, "Which Okwuekwu? We have many Okwuekwus in our clan of Umuisagba." If you then said, "But it is Okwuekwu Oda that I am looking for," your listeners would understand who you meant, and would point to one large hut that formed part of a group of smaller huts round a courtyard. The front of this hut faced the Eke market, right in line with the stalls of the sponge-sellers from Ewulu.

In Okwuekwu's hut now anxiety hung very much in the air.

"Father," the older boy observed thoughtfully, "should not one of us stay at home today just in case Mother needs help?"

Okwuekwu was not given the chance to answer. Umeadi had heard them talking and she came from the inner sleeping place where she had spent an uncomfortable night, though not uncomfortable enough to warrant her menfolk staying behind to look after her. What good would that do, she asked herself? They couldn't help her in having the child, a child that might not even survive for more than a few minutes. So why make them lose a day's work?

"Your father's wealth is the greatest," she said to her husband by way of greeting. (Everybody, every family in Ibuza had a special praise name and greeting; even slaves and those of slave ancestry took the greetings of their masters after a while.)

"She who is on a mountain of money," Okwuekwu replied, as he puffed at his now filled pipe, "we were just wondering about you...."

"I know. I heard you. Why should you stay away from the farm, and then from the court, just because I am having a baby? Are there no women in our clan any more? Have I become a coward who cannot give birth to a child? Go to the farm, and hurry. I can sense the sun coming out."

16

The boys greeted their mother, took out the farm baskets and cutlasses and hurried outside.

Okwuekwu lingered by the doorway. "If you need more help than the old women of the village can give, you know where to go, don't you?"

"Yes, I do. I may not have the child today anyway, Okwuekwu."

However if she believed that, she was wrong; or perhaps she knew otherwise but did not wish to alarm her family unduly.

As soon as the sun was settled at one side of the sky, at that angle where you know it is no longer morning and yet it is too early to be regarded as noon, Umeadi knew it was time to lay down the banana leaves she had cut earlier on and have her child. Luckily she was able to call for assistance from Ukabegwu's wife, who had stayed home because it was her time of month when she was under *nso*. She was the only help available, so Umeadi had to come out into the open compound to have her child, since an "unclean" woman was never allowed into the hut of a man with the *Alo* title. Okwuekwu had such a title.

So, with Umeadi kneeling on the damp banana leaves in front of her husband's hut, bearing down gently, with Ukabegwu's wife's hands outstretched to catch the baby and the sharp hearth knife between her teeth, a little baby girl yelled her way into this world.

Ukabegwu's wife lowered the child gently, and cut the cord. "Oh, dear, Umeadi, what have you done again? You have a daughter, and you know daughters never stay with you. I am sorry."

Umeadi lay back on the leaves and shut her eyes, thinking as she heard the child crying lustily that it would soon stop and close its eyes in death. She might as well lie there in the caressing early sun, while someone else was around to help, and regain a little energy before deciding on what to do next. But while both women sat there, and Ukabegwu's wife brought out some boiled yam which they ate, the child did not die.

"Umeadi, you'd better get up," remarked Ukabegwu's wife. "Your *ogbanje*, this visitor, looks as if she is staying this time. She is crying out with hunger. Why not put her to your breast?"

Umeadi did as she was told and, as it became apparent that the child might indeed live, her mind went to all the sacrifices she had made to her *chi*, the personal god to whom every Ibuza individual appealed in time of trouble. Her loss of daughters had continued for so many years, however, that Umeadi had reconciled herself to the fact that maybe that was her lot. Now the new baby suckled

17

with so much force, she was convinced there was some life in this one.

She handed the baby to Ukabegwu's wife, and ran as fast as her health would allow to the house of her dibia, the native doctor, who said to her:

"Your child will stay this time if you tie her with safety charms. These must consist of cowries, tops of tins brought here by the Potokis, and real bells made from metal. You see, she has an agreement with her friends in the land of the dead, to keep coming and mocking you. But this time she seems impressed by your hospitality and wants to remain here as long as she can. It is our duty to make her stay as long as possible, until she is grown enough to reject her friends. Then they will no longer have any effect on her."

Though Umeadi's heart was beating fast in excitement and fear, she managed to ask, "How old must she be before she can stop wearing the charms?"

The dibia, with a head like a skull, eyes deep in a narrow face, and the few teeth he had blackened by tobacco, chanted to himself for a while; then he seemed to come to an agreement with himself.

"Much depends on the child. Between the ages of four and seven she should be able to say, 'Go away. I am happy here. I don't want to belong to your world.' The charms are to help her frighten these evil friends away. When she moves the bells will ring, the tin metal will rattle, the cowries will rumble, and then her friends from the other world will run away, for they will never have seen anything like that before. If you want this casual visitor to stay and be a permanent member of your household, to be your daughter, you will see to it that your husband gets someone to go to Idu for him to get this copper metal which the Potokis give the king of Idu in exchange for the human slaves they buy. My payment is a white cock and a bag of cowries; and when he returns with the charms I shall tie them to your *ogbanje* myself."

Umeadi ran back as fast as she could. She was still in her prime, despite her many pregnancies; her skin, the colour of a burnt cocoa bean — not ebony black like that of Okwuekwu — was taut and shiny. She was not at all fat, but was a narrow, long-legged woman whose figure bordered on skinniness. From her father she had inherited long, goat-like legs and a neck that looped as she ran like that of a frightened giraffe. Her father, who was now dead, had been a professional runner in his day; whenever there had been a war between tribes, he had been sent to carry messages, spy how the

18

enemy's land lay, or be a pilot ambassador for the arrival of some more important personage.

Umeadi too was a great runner, and she ran now, not caring that she was still losing heavily from the recent birth. In common with most Ibuza women, she treated the event in a very straightforward manner, requiring none of the modern paraphernalia that now attends the birth of a child. A pregnant Ibuza woman would simply always carry a cooking knife with her, just in case she gave birth to her baby on her way to or from the market or farm. If she were lucky, she might have someone with her who could cut the cord; if not, she would cut the cord herself, rest a while, put her new baby on her back and thread her way home. As a result, many people bore names such as Uzo Onitsha — "born on the way to Onitsha market" — and Nwa Oboshi — "born on the way to the Oboshi river".

When Umeadi arrived home, she sent a male runner to go to inform her husband of the good news. Okwuekwu had just come to the court from his farm, after settling his sons to work, when the runner told him of the birth of his daughter, and the possibility that she would live. Girl children were not normally particularly prized creatures, but Okwuekwu had lost so many that they now assumed a quality of preciousness.

"So she has at last decided to stay with us, this regular visitor who has been visiting for a long time. Ogbanje Ojebeta: that will be her name, even though it is not very decorative. Only let her live. . . ." Okwuekwu communicated with himself as he took giant strides from the court to his compound by the Eke market.

His happiness was diluted a little when his wife told him all the native medicine man had said. Most of the visiting relatives agreed with the dibia that the only place to get the necessary charms was Idu. Okwuekwu did not at first know what to do. If he went himself, his farm, his court job and maybe his family would suffer, for who knew what fate might befall him. Yet the journey was too important to him, the responsibility too great to entrust it to somebody else. Idu, Idu . . . he had heard about the place before in Ibuza folklore.

Idu was the native mythological name for the old Benin empire. This empire was portrayed as being at the end of the world in most of the traditional stories told in Ibuza to the young and old alike on the golden moonlight nights that were one of the bounties nature bestowed upon the people of this area. To get to Idu, it was believed you would have to pass seven lands and swim or row your canoe through seven seas. It was a long way to go to Idu. Idu was said to be situated at that point where the blue sky touched the earth, sealing it up in a neat compact. The people of Idu were the last humans you would see before you came to the end of the world.

He was a great king, this king of Idu, known to the Ibuza people as the Oba Idu. History, when it was written much, much later, indentified these rulers of Benin as the Akenzuwas. But at the time when Ogbanje Ojebeta was born, there was little division between myth and reality. The trekking distance was vast, and the road dangerous: if you were caught along these bush tracks you were either killed as a human sacrifice to one of the king's innumerable gods or, if you were lucky, you would be sold to the pale-skinned "Potokis" (as all white people at that time were called; it was only much later that those living in the hinterland realised that the Portuguese had long since given way to the English, who brought with them a hypocritical kind of Christianity).

All Okwuekwu Oda knew for sure at the time was that no journey was too hazardous to make in order to ensure the life of this little girl of his. He pondered sometimes about this great Oba Idu whose chief wife, they said, was also a chief witch and priestess. Normally witches in Idu were cast away to live apart from other human beings, where they were left to fend for themselves until they died, miserably, as befitted any witch; but the big king kept his chief wife, to guard him and tell him who his enemies were. In addition, he had four hundred or so young wives who helped take care of the king. The courtyard and compound built for his wives were said to be as large as the whole town of Ibuza, and the compound formed by the king's warriors and their families as large as Ibuza and Ogwashi put together. One could recognise these royal women by their hairstyles and their heavy anklets. Their hair was plaited upwards, looking like piles of dry twigs with the pointed ends sticking up in the direction of the heavens; it was a style that narrowed their otherwise broad faces and displayed the full shape of their invariably beautiful eyes and full lips for all to see. The king would never dream of making an ugly girl his wife. Round their necks these women wore rows of colourful beads and shiny brass anklets at their feet. The king also had a group of youths who worked in the palace as staff bearers. These young men had their heads shaved, wore neat loin cloths and they too had beads round their necks, but their anklets were usually made from elephant tusks, for in those days

20

in Idu elephants were plentiful, before they were all hunted and killed off.

So renowned was this king that peoples from all regions of the world came to trade with him. The Potokis came to buy slaves, the Gambaris from the north came to sell their captives, Ibos came to sell ivory and sometimes to sell those members of their societies who had committed sins abominable.

It was a fearful kingdom, the kingdom of Idu. And Okwuekwu Oda was determined to go there.

No one knew how he survived the journey. But Okwuekwu brought the charms for his child. He did not talk much of the glory of Idu; maybe at that time he saw only the shambles of past glory, for after the famous Benin massacre of 1897, when the king was sent into exile, the entire kingdom was for a long while very unsettled.

The dibia was pleased with Okwuekwu's perseverance. He sang some incantations over the charms made from copper pieces, and together with some cowries these were strung like beads and tied round each small arm of baby Ogbanje Ojebeta. So whenever she cried and moved her arms about, the metal bells would ring, the cowries would rumble, and her friends from the other world would run, for they had never seen anything like it before, not even in the land of the dead where they were said to live.

Thus Ojebeta remained in the land of the living, with her mother Umeadi, her father Okwuekwu Oda, and her two brothers, close by the Eke market. She was cherished and marked with special tattooes, and she thrived and grew, and had to make annual visits to the dibia at Ezukwu who adjusted her charms as she grew from babyhood to girlhood.

2 "Felenza"

Umeadi stood in the market talking animatedly to a group of other women, most of whom were known to her little girl Ogbanje Ojebeta who sat by the doorway to her father's hut, watching the group studiously. They looked very concerned and worried. The usual clamour of the Eke market was subdued. It was apparent that all was far from well.

Ojebeta watched for a while, feeling disinclined to go and play with her friends, and then she called out: "Mother, Mother, come here. I want to have a suck."

Her mother looked at her, did not smile, but decided to ignore her call and went on talking to her friends. Funny, though, that none of them was laughing, thought the little girl.

The sun was still glowing but it was halfway down the sky on its way to its night's repose. The Eke market was usually very busy with haggling people, dressed in bright cloths, all laughing, gossiping and talking. But this evening there were not many people; those there stood talking in groups with arms folded across their chests as if they were cold. The stall of the sponge-sellers from Ewulu was almost empty. The few of them who had come were now on the verge of going home.

Ojebeta was puzzled about what could have gone wrong. In angry frustration she called out again, now louder than she had done previously: "Mother, I want a suck!"

Umeadi heard her, noted the agitation in her voice and stopped talking, then said something to her friends and they tried to laugh; but it was unhappy, ghostly laughter. Not the usual kind of laughter that used to set her ashake with near hysterical joy. Ojebeta could bear it no longer, so she ran, the bell charms on her arms ringing behind her.

Without losing her composure, her mother scooped her up and

gave her a flat breast to suck. She let Ojebeta catch the nipple like a plug, and murmured, "I hope my *chi* preserves me for you." It was an appeal to her personal god to save her from some impending disaster threatening her; the universal god, Olisa, took care of group calamities.

Ojebeta heard it, but was too busy enjoying the warmth and nearness of her mother's body. It reminded her of when her mother used to carry her on her back to the stream and sometimes to the market, though she had stopped doing that now; people had started to make fun of her, saying that she was too big to be carried like that, and that it was high time she allowed her mother to have another baby. Ojebeta did not like those busybodies, telling her that as if she knew where little brothers and sisters came from. She found it difficult, though, to give up breast-sucking. Her mother did not discourage it; her father Okwuekwu Oda even encouraged it. He would say to himself: "Is there another child on the way, that I should not let the only daughter who would stay with me suck at her mother's breasts as long as she likes? Let her suck; maybe that will help her realise how much we love and want her. Did I not make a dangerous journey to Idu, the land where people still sell men in slavery or kill them as sacrifices, just to keep her alive? So let her suck."

And Ojebeta was not reprimanded, even though she was now coming up to the age of six full years. It was one of the ways her mother showed her affection, for she seemed to be getting soft as middle age drew closer.

Down the road on the Umuodafe side a family was approaching, coming to the market for the second burial of their dead. The deceased man had not been very old; and his children, some of whom were still infants, had come to the market now. Second burials were usually big affairs, with music and dancing, the mourners inviting as many dancers from their own age-groups as they could afford; the noisier a second Eke burial was, the higher the prestige of the family. But this one was like a group of youngsters playing at funerals. The older people could not forgive the dead young father for going so soon and suddenly and leaving his poor wife behind to care for his babies, babies who were too young to invite their age-groups to accompany them to the market (age-groups, made up of those born within the same three-year period, were like mutual benefit societies, whose members, from adolescence, would organise meetings and dances for important occasions such as this). But that was not the only reason why this particular ceremony was

23

so subdued. Another reason was that it made every man, woman and child in Ibuza think quickly about themselves, their future and their fate.

It was still a rumour, but one which would be confirmed when the town's runner who had been sent down to Isele Azagba returned: that there was a kind of sudden death spreading in that area. The people of Ibuza did not know what sort of death it was or whether or not it was caused by some infectious disease. All anyone knew was that it was happening. Had not the stall of the people from the town of Isele Azagba been empty today? They never missed Eke market day, coming to Ibuza with their giant baskets packed full with red peppers, which they sold there and on the way back home bought cakes of salt and red Ibuza palm oil — yet today their stall was empty.

When the rumour had first reached the ears of many Ibuza people, all noise, joyous music and all kinds of loud cries were stopped until the rumour was fully investigated. That this dead man had to have his second burial today was a double sadness. The family could not change the date, for if the children did not come to the market to perform this ceremony for their father then their mother could not come out of mourning. It was very necessary for her to come out of her seven-month period of mourning in order to be able to fetch water to look after her children, to be able to choose another husband, and in fact to be able to live again. Who knew whether, when the rumours were confirmed, things might not become even worse? So it was essential to have it over and done with, rather quickly.

Umeadi and her little group of sad-faced women walked into the Eke market to greet the bereaved children, and as they prayed for them the women all wept quietly.

"May the spirit of your dead father guard you," they said, and touched the heads of the children and gave each a few cowries. The children's people thanked them as they moved along to the end of the market, saying the praise names of the dead man, rather than singing them as was the usual custom.

"There is some truth in the saying that we die as we live," Ozubu, the plump wife of Nwadei, remarked as she watched the sorrowful group move away.

Her listeners nodded in silence.

"Nwosisi was a quiet man," observed Umeadi. "He would not walk in the middle of the road, but always by the side so that he would not have to talk to anybody. He was so shy — even in death.

24

Have you ever seen a second burial as quiet as this? Have you ever heard of anyone choosing a time like this for his second burial?"

The other women shook their heads. The general belief was that this man Nwosisi could have chosen differently had he wanted to; he had elected to die quietly, to announce his death in the big Eke market as unobtrusively as possible.

Ozubu concluded the discussion by noting, "Do you know that the day he died he was lying facing the wall as if sleeping? People thought he was still resting. He did not even want his parents who were in the next room to know he was dying. He knew what he was doing, going away like that, leaving his old parents alive and his young children uncared for. Olisa save us from such men as this one."

They all rejoined with their amen: "*Ise.*"

Despite the looming rumour, the women knew that they still had their families to look after. They still had to buy things from the market here to sell at the Ogbeogonogo market in Asaba in two days' time. Umeadi was the first to break the group.

"I must go to the stalls of those Igbo men selling kernels. I haven't got enough to press for my oil to take to Asaba market," she said, putting Ojebeta down and remonstrating with her mildly. "You must learn to walk on your own two feet, you know."

The others smiled in spite of themselves, and Ozubu said jokingly, "No, she will not. Haven't you heard what she told her little friend Nkadi, that she will take you with her when she gets married?"

They all laughed briefly, and Ojebeta covered her face as she ran preceding her mother to the kernel sellers' stalls, her waist beads jingling with her safety charms. Those watching her as she went knew that she was a loved child, over-decorated with trinkets and expensive tattoos.

"Pom! Pom! Pom! The rumours that have been going round are true. Pom! There is a kind of death coming from across the salty waters. It has killed many people in Isele Azagba, it is creeping to Ogwashi, it is now coming to us. They call it Felenza. It is white man's death. They shoot it into the air, and we breathe it in and die. Pom! Pom. . . ."

People, some on the verge of eating their evening meal, some still thudding their yam for the meal in their wooden mortars, listened helplessly as the gongman went round Ibuza with his unwelcome news. The town's runner must have returned. He must have told his tale of woe to the diokpa, the oldest man, then there must have been consultation among the elders and it must have been decided that the whole town should be warned. Everybody felt a kind of chill; not that an epidemic was anything new to the people of Ibuza, but at least previously they had always known what measures to take to avert mass disaster. They had experienced diseases like smallpox, which was so feared that they gave it the name of "Nna ayin" — "Our Father" — for at that time smallpox meant death; they knew that to stop it spreading throughout the villages any victim had to be isolated, so when somebody was attacked he would be taken into the bush and left there to die. All his worldly possessions would be burned, and no one would be allowed to mourn for him. So much feared was smallpox.

But this felenza was a new thing that the "Potokis" had shot into the air, though everyone wondered why.

"We have done them no wrong," people said. "They came to places like Benin and Bonny, bought healthy slaves from our people and paid us well. And this is how they thank us."

Rumour had it that some Europeans had been killed in Benin (Okwuekwu was one of those who carried the rumour when he returned from Idu with the copper charms for his daughter); but they had had their revenge at the time by killing many of the people there and exiling the rightful king of Idu. Why send them this kind of death now? The people of Ibuza pondered, speculated and hoped that it would never come to them, for where were they to run to?

But soon it came to Ogwashi, and within days men started dropping down dead on their farms. Death was always so sudden that the relatives were too shocked to cry.

Ojebeta's father, the strong man Okwuekwu Oda, was one of the first to be hit. She remembered that morning he had come to where she was still sleeping by the wood fire: it was the harmattan season and mornings inside the hut were chilly at that time of year.

"You did not take the *adu* I brought you from the farm yesterday," he said to her. "Here it is. Roast it for your morning meal."

She had scrambled up and greeted him with his praise names that meant "your father's wealth is the greatest" — *"Aku nna yi ka."* He had returned her greeting, enquiring how she was that morning and whether she had slept well. She had nodded. As she watched her mother fill his pipe for him and light it she heard her say:

"If the head is so bad, stay at home today."

Her father had snapped: "Cowards fear death. It can catch up with you anywhere, whether you're lying down on your sleeping mat or digging in your farm. I don't want to die lying down like a crochety old man. I am going to the farm. Besides, who told you headaches mean felenza?"

With that he stalked out puffing angrily at his pipe as he went, smoke from the pipe following him like a line of mist.

That was the last time Ojebeta saw her father on his feet; she could still hear his footfall as he marched away in indignation. He came back in the evening, but carried by some people. He had died. Felenza had killed him on his farm.

After that it seemed to Ojebeta's young mind that the whole world was dying, one by one. Her father's hut was pulled to the ground and a mourning hut was quickly constructed for her mother. Her brothers by then were big men in their own right with bachelor huts. When felenza was at its height her eldest brother decided to leave home in search of a European job; he would rather go and face whatever fate awaited him in an unknown place than stay in Ibuza waiting for felenza to come to him.

Only her brother Okolie remained. He was a handsome man like their father and had already joined the Uloko dance which was an important dance for their age-group — so far the epidemic had not touched this age-group so much as older people's. They hoped that most of them would be able to survive it anyway.

This speculation was buttressed by the fact that after a month the crisis seemed to have passed. It was then that Ibuza began to hear explanations of what had caused the disease. Before that time most people living in the interior of Nigeria did not know that the whole country now belonged to the people called the British who were ruling them indirectly through the local chiefs and elders. Now, in the year of 1916, the rumours said that the new colonial masters were at war with their neighbours "the Germanis"; and the latter fought the British by blowing poisonous gas into the air. When you breathed it in, you died. Many inside Ibuza were asking themselves what they had to do with the Germanis, and the Germanis with them. There was no one to answer their questions; even the diokpas did not know the answers. They consoled themselves by making innumerable offerings of goats and chickens in the hope that their god Olisa would be well placated and would protect them.

Umeadi mourned for her husband, and whenever Okolie could take time off from his dance practice he would come and fetch water for his widowed mother, for while in mourning she was forbidden to visit the stream, to bathe, to enter any hut where the man of the family had a title. In fact a woman in mourning was not really expected to survive long after the death of her husband, though miraculously many widows did, perhaps because most wives were very much younger than their husbands and had that built-in resistance which only youth and a determination to live can provide. And Umeadi like many another woman might have survived had not her resistance been lowered by the very gas that killed her husband.

Although Ojebeta never heard her mother complain of any headaches, as her father had, she had become very aware of Death — that somebody who could take away your loved ones with little warning. Her father had gone, though relatives assured her that he still kept good watch over her when she was asleep; Ojebeta would have preferred him to be around as before, but she could no longer bargain. She clung the more to her mother, sucking at Umeadi's milkless breasts and when she was not about sucking at her own fingers. There seemed to be so many women in mourning like her mother, wearing smoked rags, that one would have thought this felenza was only a killer of men.

One morning, misty and damp, a fine rain was being blown from among the giant iroko trees that stood majestically in the middle of the market. The wind was strong enough to toss all the bits of dried leaves about and shake Umeadi's makeshift mourning hut. It even blew at the last embers of the fire in the hut. Ojebeta crawled near her mother for warmth, reassurance and protection. Her feet and body were covered with clay from the floor which was not beaten down well enough to stop the mud from coming off and smearing one. Ojebeta did not mind. Where her mother lay, there was security, and Ojebeta called out to her in the gentle tone she found herself using recently, since her father's death. Something of her, she did not know what, seemed to have been buried with him. She had become more thoughtful, so much so that many a time now her mother would ask what it was she was thinking about. Startled, she would say quickly, "Nothing, Mother."

She called gently again and when there was no response guessed that her mother was still asleep. It was no wonder her mother slept late these days, for there was nowhere for her to go, no kernels for her to press to make oil, no cassava for her to fetch. She was confined to her hut like a prisoner until her months of mourning were over. Maybe after that, things would go back to being almost as they used to be before the arrival of that horrible gas that took her dear father away. Ojebeta snuggled closer to the nipple of her mother's sagging breast. The wind went on and on, but she was no longer frightened. Her mother was there by her, so no harm could come to her now. She fell asleep.

She was startled by a voice wailing and shouting as if hell had been let loose. Then a strong pair of hands was lifting her from the mud floor on which she was lying beside her mother. The hands were those of her brother Okolie, and he too was crying. So was her mother's friend Ozubu.

Ojebeta rubbed the sleep from her eyes and saw that Ozubu was carrying a calabash of cassava pulp which she had just brought from her farm. It had been intended as a gift for Umeadi; but now the calabash was left on the floor, and they were crying and shaking their heads. The loud noises they were making had attracted near neighbours and relatives. Her father's sister, who normally was not on speaking terms with her mother, was now leading Ojebeta away from her brother, at the same time reminding them all that they were not supposed to make so much noise while the present trouble was still about. She was not herself being very successful in this, however, for she was crying too.

By now Ojebeta understood. Her mother Umeadi had gone too, had been taken away from her by the same felenza.

When the moon was just about to come out, and the day's wind had stopped blowing, and those who could eat had eaten, and the night insects were beginning to make themselves heard, Ojebeta watched her mother's hut burning. She saw Uteh, her father's sister, cleaning some of her mother's utensils, and although she appeared to have lost interest in everything Ojebeta asked:

"Why are you washing them, big mother?"

"To be buried with your mother. She will need them to cook for your father in the land of the dead. Look, I have even filled a big calabash with soap for her, so that she will never lack any."

"Why did she leave me behind with no one to look after me?"

Uteh held her tightly and wept all over her, shaking her long black feet in silent agony.

"You belong to the land of the living, Ogbanje Ojebeta," she said.

3 A Short Journey

It was still dark when they started on their winding, red-earthed journey to Onitsha. The late night stars had withdrawn from above and were now well hidden behind the tangled foliage of trees and the looming clouds. The grey mist of dawn lay so heavily upon the horizon that it was impossible to see beyond a few yards.

The silence was profound. The night animals had gone into hiding and the day ones were still reluctant to come out into the open to start their early morning business. Ojebeta and her brother were not unaware of the animals' sleepy movements in the thick walls of the green forest as the subdued noise of their footsteps startled one or two creatures into temporary wakefulness. Except for these minor signs of activity, there was stillness everywhere. As they padded through the bush tracks, they seemed to be entering the very belly of the earth. It was as if they were being gradually but nonetheless determinedly swallowed by a dark, mysterious, all-green world, the walls of which were enveloping them, fencing them in, closing them up. Overhead hung the tangled branches of huge tropical trees, on both sides of them were large leaves, creeping plants and enormous tree-trunks, all entwined together to form this impenetrable dark green grove.

The foot track they were following was like a thin red snake hemmed in by the two sides of this green presence so that they could not even see its head, because that end was blocked by the meeting of the two green walls ahead.

By the time they had passed all the huts, their red earth track was fast thinning into a mere bush path. Still they padded, and without speaking. The silence of their surroundings had affected Ojebeta somewhat. Gone were her usual bird-like prattles, her bat-like bumping into things, her teasing of adults. She felt that she was in the presence of a Power mysterious. She felt that she was being watched by that hushed, hidden someone. Had she ever been taught how, her reaction might have been to kneel and pray to that lurking Power who had made the plants so lush, the animals so quiet, the stars so retiring. But she was not Christian; neither was her big brother Okolie, though she sensed his need for silence now too, and knew somehow that the feeling was mutual. She tried hard, and effectively, to subdue the jangling sounds made by the little bells and the empty tobacco tins tied round her arms.

The trekked for what seemed ages until they came to the stream. Here at least they were in the presence of something moving. Clear, glistening water tumbled among tiny rocks and washed the small green plants by the bank. The fact that the area was a kind of clearing which allowed a direct view of the sky, a gap in the green canopy, added to the feeling of openness.

"We must wash," Okolie said, and ran down the slope that led to the stream without looking behind him to find out if his sister was following. His voice, even to himself, sounded alien and unused.

The movements of the waters made the stream sparkle like the pieces of imitation silver their mother used to buy from Onitsha on big market days. Ojebeta remembered being told how those shiny bits of metal were brought there from Bonny and from Benin, and it was said that they were brought by some people from across the sea.

She gazed at the undergrowth, all bright and fresh, at the water that splashed over jutting rocks and small stones, and at the silvery-white sands in the bathing areas where there were no pebbles. It all looked so pure and so clean, cleaner than she could ever have imagined possible at the usually very busy Atakpo stream. She was so taken aback by the purity of it all that she hated to disturb it by wading in to have a wash. Encouraged by her brother's voice, she asked the question that all of a sudden formed in her mind.

"Why is the water so pure and clean?" Her voice was rather loud, and a nearby frog protested by starting to croak furiously, so much so that it awakened several others who joined in the chorus until the stream was filled with the croaky wailings of frogs.

Okolie looked at her accusingly as if to say, "See what you have done?" Nonetheless he replied patiently to her question. "It is because there is no one about yet. We are the first people to disturb its calm."

She thought about this answer for a while and was puzzled at its correctness. Why, had not her mother, her friends, even all the professional storytellers of Ibuza told her that when they and all humans were asleep the people of the dead — Ndi-Nmo — took over? They came to the stream at night to wash themselves and their clothes, just like the living humans did in the day. And when the first cock crowed, they disappeared and returned to their natural habitat, the land of the dead. If that was so, thought Ojebeta, surely they would have left the stream a little disturbed?

"What of the people of the dead?" she piped now. "They must have been using the stream all night, when we were sleeping. I know that my mother and all those people killed off by the felenza cannot go one day without having a bath. Surely Mother must have been to have her daily bath, even though she has died? I saw the burial. They put all her cooking pots and washing calabashes in her burial mat. My big mother Uteh even put a great calabash of soap in it, so that Mother wouldn't lack any."

Her brother stopped in his tracks, looked at Ojebeta thoughtfully and said reassuringly: "The people of the dead are not as dirty and noisy as we are. The don't go about disturbing the peace or stirring up mud. They float, almost like birds." Then he added, with a little authority, and indicating that he would rather not be asked any more questions on the subject, "Have your bath: I'm going to the men's bathing place. You must hurry."

With that he waded his way noisily across the shallow stream, stirring up more of the otherwise peaceful mud in his wake so that there was a distinctive cloudy line behind him. He disappeared deeper into the green enclosure of the trees, several of which had branches that hung over and across the stream and joined with branches from trees on the other side, as if in perpetual handshake.

Ojebeta stood wondering what it would be like to go into the men's bathing place. She would have liked a glimpse of what it was that the men kept there in such a secret place. Why did they have to go so deep into the dark belly of the forest to bathe, when women and children made do with this open place where the sand was clean and the water clear and shallow? She was not particularly keen on having her bath so early in the morning when almost all the rest of the world was still asleep. Where were they going anyway to warrant this secrecy, this early rising from their sleeping mats? Her brother had simply told her that they were going to see a relative of theirs living in Onitsha.

She had heard her mother mention this female relative once or twice, but it had been too vague for young Ojebeta to make out to which side of the family this person actually was related. All she knew was that this relative had had the effrontery to marry not only outside the town of Ibuza but completely outside her tribe. They said she married a man who came from over the salty waters. It was bad enough for an Ibuza woman to marry someone from Ogwashi or from Asaba, but when you went beyond that and married someone who did not even speak the Ibo language, then you were regarded as lost or even sold into slavery.

So now they were going to see this otherwise lost relative, but why? As Ojebeta waded reluctantly into the stream, she thought of the bad luck that had caused her to lose both her mother and father within such a short period of time. Involuntarily tears of self-pity and frustration welled up in her eyes, dropped down her cheeks and then into the morning water. There were so many things she wanted answers to; but she sensed that her brother, who was now her most frequent companion, was too preoccupied with his own private problems to listen to her. Quite often these days he snapped at her and told her that her questions were childish. So she had begun holding conversations with her mother — had she not been told that the dead do see? — especially when she was as puzzled as she felt now.

"Why, Mother, am I going to see this woman — this Ma Palagada, or whatever her name is? She never came to visit us, not even when Father was alive. Why should I go to see her now, and maybe stay with her? I don't want to stay away from home, away from where you and Father were buried. Mother, Father, answer me, both of you, please. . . ."

She listened with both ears and with breath abated, but apart from the half-hearted early songs of birds and the now slowly rising croaks of frogs and the buzzing of water insects, there was no answer. Instead her brother's head showed itself from the grove like the head of a tortoise coming out of its shell. He shouted at her, crossly:

"When will you start your wash? We're going to Onitsha, you know, not to the farm."

Quickly she threw her small cloth onto the bank, cupped some water over her body and began to rub herself with her palm. Okolie's patience was by now exhausted, and he came towards her hurriedly knotting his loin cloth like someone preparing for a fight, bent down to scoop up some sand from the bottom of the stream, and walked up to her.

34

"Bend down," he said rather impatiently.

She obeyed at once, noting the irritation in his voice. He poured the fine sand on to her back and rubbed it gently all over, so that it pleasantly scratched the prickly heat rashes on her dark skin. Then he poured the cool water over her, and this gave her a refreshing feeling and she giggled. She sat deep in the water, wanting him to play with her. But he did not. He simply rinsed her newly shone hair which had been specially cut for this journey and said,

"Ojebeta, we must hurry. Do you hear me? We must hurry." He looked about him for a few seconds, then exclaimed, "Look, I can see the sun peeping through the leaves already. It is going to be a very hot day."

She looked in the direction where his finger was pointing and saw a new morning glow, whose seeming suddeness surprised her. Only minutes before it had been misty and grey, and now here was this golden sunshine lighting the little openings between the trees. She also noticed that now it was not only her friend the croaking frog that was awake; all things about her seemed infused with life. Various bush animals were trying out their morning voices; a bird or two began a song, to be answered from other hidden nests, until it all rose into a crescendo of sweet forest sounds, a kind of avalanche of musical calls.

He was right, her brother. If they were going to Onitsha, they should be on their way. She had never been there herself, though from what she had often heard her mother say, it could not be too far. Her mother when she used to go had to spend sufficient time there to sell her plantains and the palm oil she invariably had pressed from kernels the night before; but Ojebeta and her brother would not need to stay very long, for they had nothing to sell.

After her wash, Okolie picked up her small *npe* waist cloth which she had left by the bank, and after shaking off the clinging grass tied it round her. When she smiled her thanks, watching him tie his *otuogwu* in his usual toga fashion, he looked at her but did not return her smile. She sensed that all was not well in his mind but did not ask what. Even if he had told her of his financial worries, she would not have understood. Once more they resumed their path in silence.

The sun was now completely out, glowing bright in the sky. The silvery drops of water that had sparkled on the leaves like pieces of metal were now beginning to dry. Soon they came to an area where the bush track gradually widened, and instead of walls of green forest there was a sea of giant grass, dotted with a few cassava farms. The dazzling sunshine almost blinded Ojebeta, and she lagged behind, so that her brother was forced to slow down his big strides in order for her to catch up with him.

"Come, little sister, I will carry you on my shoulders," he said with concern.

She shook her head defiantly, implying that she was capable of walking all the way, but Okolie knew that it was a poor show of reluctance to accept his offer. He knew that her feet must indeed be aching by now, even though her pride would not let her admit it. He smiled sadly. The thought of what he was planning to do to her began to nag at his mind and torment him again, however much he tried to suppress it. He was only doing the right thing, he told himself, the only possible thing. He had no alternative. He begged their dead parents to forgive him, but what else was there for a young bachelor like himself to do with a little sister of merely seven years of age? A spoilt child who was still sucking at her mother's breast when all other children of her age had long been weaned? Mixed up with these feelings of self-justification was the conviction that he desperately needed whatever money came his way to prepare himself for his coming-of-age dance, one of the most important events in his age-group. He could not afford to do anything else. . . .

He looked at Ojebeta again and, as if in compensation for his anticipated sins, he relented his critical thoughts of her and began to address her with her praise names.

"Come on, our beautiful visitor. Who has skin like that of the beautiful wives of the king of Idu? Who is the girl with the cleanest teeth in all the seven lands of the world? Who is our mother's pet and our father's heart? Who is my only sister, who originally came as a visitor but has now decided to stay? Come. Come and ride on your big brother's shoulders, like the queen of the gods on her horse that is part human and part animal. Come!"

He stooped down for her like a man in deep supplication. His *otuogwu* spread right out as if it were the wing of a black guiding angel. The morning sun, rising behind him, added a heavenly touch of benevolence to the picture he made, kneeling there, beckoning his sister.

"Come," he begged again.

She could no longer refuse. She ran into the protection of his wide arms. He gathered her into his *otuogwu* and his thin red lips spread

36

into a sad smile as he hugged her on to his shoulder.

For that split second there was laughter, the type of happy laughter she used to know but which now seemed very rare: spontaneous and full of hope. It lasted for a brief moment, while her brother swung her from one broad shoulder to the other, until he made a pad on one of them with the knot of his cloth, for her to sit on with comfort. He walked quickly, galloping like a mighty horse, not very much aware of the plump little girl he was carrying away to be sold.

The sun was now directly overhead, and Okolie sweated as he covered the last few miles before boarding the canoe that would ferry them across the river to Onitsha. His sister had grown tired of talking to him from where she was sitting on his shoulder and had fallen asleep, exhausted by the length of the journey and by the fact that she had had no morning meal at all. Still Okolie hurried, the thudding sound of his footfall like that of his father before him. He too was becoming hungry, and although by the time he got to Ogbogonogo in Asaba the early food-sellers were already hawking themselves hoarse he decided not to delay. He must catch one of the early canoes owned by the Ijaws which were used to ferry market women on their way to the big Onitsha market.

By Cable Point, he was busy speculating about how much he was going to ask this relative, now very distant, to pay for Ogbanje Ojebeta. He had never sold anyone before, and now he persuaded himself that what he was about to do was not selling in its actual sense. He was giving his sister away into the keeping of this rich lady, and getting some money for her so that, when she grew up, she might be given to a suitable husband and could collect the bride price. Okolie was not unaware of the fact that he was not the eldest of his father's two sons, but he reasoned to himself, "Where is Owezim now? He left when the felenza was at its height, and I alone was the one who had to gather up our father when he died; I alone had to cover our mother's nakedness when she lay there dead on the mud floor. So I deserve to have the money I need so badly for my coming-of-age dance. What does it matter if I have to trade my sister to get it? She will be well looked after there, better than I can afford to do in Ibuza. Let her go. This is the only way she can survive and grow into adulthood."

Another thought crossed his mind then. Suppose his sister was

37

sold into slavery to the Potokis, and they took her away across the seas and he never saw her again? He deadened his conscience and reminded himself that the new white men who were now penetrating into their small towns and villages were trying hard to abolish that type of trade. People were not going missing as before. Okolie recollected how in his childhood many young women had been kidnapped in the middle of the night when they went out to their toilet. He could still remember his grandfather coming home with strings of captives after raiding neighbouring villages; some of the captives — the lucky ones — were kept as house slaves, but most of them were either taken down to Bonny or sold to people going to Idu. Those were the times when the human market was at its height. Not now. Nobody would dream of treating this little sister of his that way, because she was special. If it occurred to him that so might the little girls his grandfather had captured in other villages have been special to their people, Okolie stifled the idea. He had now worked his guilty conscience up to such an extent that he found himself running, hurrying to get it over with and forget about it. Life, he said under his breath to himself, is a chance. Ogbanje Ojebeta was now being offered a chance to make the best of her life.

"What is all this hurry and talking to yourself for so early in the day? I have been watching your approach and could not believe my eyes that it was you. And where are you carrying your sister to? Is she not well?"

Okolie in his rush and self-analysis had not seen his in-law Eze coming towards him. In fact he had deliberately set out from Ibuza early to avoid meeting market women whom he knew would start asking questions and maybe offering to take Ojebeta from him — though they would not have given him any money for her, which was what he wanted most. And if he dreaded meeting the Ibuza market women, the worst person on earth he could come across was this in-law of his.

Like many of their sex, the sons of Okwuekwu and their father himself when he was alive did not think much of this man who had had the audacity to marry a girl from their family. After all, Uteh was a beauty; and not only was she a beauty, but she was a daughter born along the Eke market. Yet she had condescended to marry this man with brown skin and eyes that watered all the time like those of wet chicks. His body was of the kind that after each bath looked as if he poured ashes over it. He was never healthy, neither in looks

38

nor in reasoning. Uteh on the other hand had the jet-black skin of the family, and a small intelligent head with a very high forehead. When she walked her heels never reached the ground, only the balls of her feet. She was always standing straight and looking over people's heads for she was tall, so narrow and her body so polished that she had the nickname of "the black snake that glides". That she had deigned to marry this fool, however, had alienated her from her blood relatives, who said she had married the most idiotic person in the whole of Ibuza.

Of course, no one actually knew what else was expected of Uteh, since her father accepted the bride price before she was able to make any choice. And what obedient daughter of any family, good or bad, would be allowed to marry a man of her choice? She was only obeying her father's instructions. Okwuekwu was then too young to have a say in such adult matters. And when the bride price was paid by her prospective husband's people, Eze too was a youth and no one knew he would grow up to have short legs, ashy skin and eyes that watered. He was kind to Uteh, and that was all she wanted. It still pained her, however, that in important family matters in which the first daughter of the house ought to have been consulted they always ruled her out.

In fact she had been thinking of taking Ojebeta as her own child, the daughter she had never had. She had borne one son, in her younger days, but had never been pregnant again since then; rumour said it was because she was so narrow that she could not carry children. However, her husband Eze was so satisfied with her that he never even thought of getting himself another wife. This was one of the reasons why people thought him stupid, that he worshipped his woman and did not wish to expand his family. What man in his right senses would entrust his whole future to one son only, and at that a son who had been pampered and spoilt by his mother? He must be a stupid man. And since his wife Uteh visited the medicine man more frequently than was considered good for any woman, who was to say she was not mixing some concoction into his food so that he would have eyes for no one but her? Did one ever see a person with such eyes that watered all the time? So people speculated.

Eze, knowing the way people regarded him, at times tended to act somewhat comically just to attract a little respect, but it was always done in such an unorthodox way that all he did for himself was to attract more ridicule. After a while, though, he stopped caring, and rested content to be himself, which meant speaking the truth as tactlessly as he liked, not minding if others laughed and called him "River Niger eye".

Now here he stood in the middle of the road and demanded to know where Okolie was going with his sleeping sister.

"We are going on a very important errand to Onitsha," faltered Okolie, "and we're in a great hurry, otherwise we shall be late for the early canoes."

Eze might have watery eyes but he did not have a watery brain. He was thinking. He screwed up his ashy face in such a way as to create a mass of lines like those formed by time. Though he was not a young man, he was by no means aged enough to have acquired such wrinkles: it was one of his comical faces. Then he spoke in a voice, again put on purposely, that sounded like a rabbit that was being strangled.

"And your little sister is part of this errand, too? I mean, is she going to say something at this urgent meeting that warranted your leaving Ibuza when everybody was still asleep?"

He looked up to him, his face still screwed up, standing with his bandy legs astride so that Okolie could not bypass him without a struggle. Okolie might be feet taller than him, but to him he was a child in arms, who was obviously not at ease with himself about this secret mission he was undertaking so early in the morning.

Okolie saw the situation. Making a clean breast of it would condemn him forever in the eyes of his people. They would stop calling him Okolie the son of Okwuekwu Oda, the best horn-blower in the Uloko age-group. They would instead call him Okolie who sold his sister for money. But he *needed* this money, he argued with himself. The only alternative to getting it this way would have been to go and steal, and that could result in anything, including death, for if you were caught stealing from another person the owner of the property could hit you with anything he could lay his hands on, even a cutlass. He did not want to work hard at farming, as most members of his age-group did to raise money for their outing preparations; not only would that take a long time but the work was too strenuous. Had not his late father always called him a good-for-nothing, with strong legs and hefty arms which he refused to put to proper use, fit only to go about blowing horn-pipes for funeral ceremonies and at bride departures? "What are those strong arms for, Okolie?" he used to ask. Often he would threaten his son, "You will not eat from the yam I worked for with my own sweat." But

40

having said that he would hasten to court to do his "Order" bit, and behind his back Okolie would convince his mother that he intended to improve his ways. His mother would relent, and give him hot pounded yam and spicy fish soup; and then Okolie would go out with his horn pipe under his cloth, in search of any celebrations in Ibuza. Now that both his parents were dead, he was left with a big farm that he did not know how to manage. Some small children had already started calling him "Okolie Ujo Ugbo" — Okolie the farm truant — for when other young men were out on their farms during the day he was seen walking about doing nothing. Sometimes he took consolation in his horn pipe, though who could enjoy blowing horn pipes when there was no audience to listen, no dancers to dance to the melody?

He would go back to the farm; but first he needed the money his sister would fetch, to see him through the beginning of another farming season and to buy a new horn pipe, and some women's head-scarves which he would have to tie round his waist for the dance. He would also need strings of cowries and little bells for his feet. Essential too were large, colourful ostrich feathers to complete his Uloko outfit. He reasoned with himself now, did anyone ever come of age twice? It happened only once in one's lifetime, and it was the duty of each person to make it as memorable as he could possibly afford. He looked again at this bandy-legged man standing in his path and his patience snapped.

"Move out of my way, you old tortoise, and let me pass."

"No, Okolie, not before you let me take Ogbanje Ojebeta to her big mother, my wife Uteh. The way you are holding her, one would think you were going to sell her or something. But no blood brother would think of doing such a thing."

Eze's way of talking artificially slowly gave Okolie time to recover from the shock of being found out in advance. Putting on a bluff, he started to laugh, so heartily that Ojebeta woke up.

"No, in-law, you know that your wife is not the only big mother she has. You remember our relative Olopo who married a Kru man? She is very rich now. They say she has built many houses in Otu at Onitsha. She heard of all the mishaps that were befalling us, with everybody dying and sent me a messenger last market day to tell me that I should bring Ojebeta to Onitsha since she wished to see her and buy her this and that, to console her for the loss of her mother. That is why we are going to her. I am hurrying now so that I can catch the Ijaw canoes, and we shall be back in Ibuza in time for

41

the evening meal. Ojebeta will stay with your wife, but first I want her to get over the loss of our mother. Remember they were so close that when she died we found Ojebeta lying across her and clinging to her breast? She has missed Mother so, haven't you?" he asked his little sister, chucking her under the chin.

Ojebeta did not answer either way. She had scrambled down and was standing beside him, still drowsy, weary from the journey and from the lack of any sustenance that morning. Noon was fast approaching.

Okolie had calculated that they would be in Onitsha before noon. What he had not taken into account was that he was going to meet bandy-legged Eze with his searching questions. In turn, Okolie would have liked to enquire what he was going to Asaba to do at such an early hour, but he did not, for the explanation might be devious, as all Eze's explanations were, and it was sure to be time-consuming as well.

Eze was thinking again, and whatever his thoughts were, they were apparently sad thoughts. He looked at Ojebeta and simply said to her: "Those who are born to survive will always survive. Your big mother will always welcome you, and the door of my hut is open always to you. The little pieces of yam you would eat would not be wanting in my hut. If you need anywhere to stay, come to us."

With that he dipped his hand into the jute hunter's bag that hung on his shoulder, brought out a piece of dried fish and gave it to her. "Take this and break your fast with it."

He walked away quickly, with no word for Okolie.

Okolie's heart sank. Should he or should he not go ahead with his plans? But who wanted to be saddled with a little seven-year-old sister? And he did not want her living with Uteh, because he did not like Eze. No, let her go to Ma Palagada, and he would collect some money from her. Ogbanje Ojebeta's fate was decided. She must be sold.

He pulled her as fast as he could and they ran the few remaining yards to the waterfront, and boarded the canoe that was to take them to the Onitsha market.

4 Onitsha Market

The Onitsha market called Otu, one of West Africa's big meeting places, was situated on the bank of the River Niger and served not only the people of Onitsha but those from the surrounding Ibo towns and villages as well. They regarded this place as the centre of their world. A market day was an occasion to dress up and meet with friends, as well as to buy and sell. The market was where people who wanted to display their dances went, be it an age-group or a family showing the end of their mourning for a departed relative. And there were many superstitions attached to the market place. For example, if a person was insane then so long as the madness was not shown in the market there was hope of a cure. The big markets were places where the visible living met and among them moved the dead and the invisible.

So Otu Onitsha was like a nerve-centre sending messages to all the surrounding areas. The latest agbada cloth was to be bought at Onitsha. The newest fashion was sure to be seen worn by somebody at Onitsha. The most recent gossip could be heard at Onitsha.

Okolie and his charge Ojebeta did not regret leaving the flat-bottomed canoe that had ferried them across the river from Asaba. At first Ojebeta had liked the enthusiastic rowing of the canoe men, so much so that she had allowed her fingers to run through the water as they sped. But after a while, when she had begun to feel dizzy, and a market woman carrying a pot of red palm oil to sell had warned her to take care lest she was thrown into the river, Ojebeta had become scared. Her fear was not lessened by the strange loud songs of the canoe men in tune with their stylish rowing. When they stopped singing, their talking was so voluble that their voices seemed to be drawing the gentle waves of the blue waters against the brown sides of the wooden boat. As they rowed near the waterside, the clamour coming from Otu Onitsha drowned all thoughts.

43

The Eke market was the biggest market Ojebeta had previously ever seen before, but this one looked to her like a whole city. It was a complete market landscape that seemed to stretch for miles. People swarmed and buzzed like insects. Most were dressed up fashionably but some, like the canoe men and the people selling fresh fish, wore only very meagre cloths wrapped kite-like round their loins. Apart from the Ibo traders, there were Yoruba stalls where you could buy different kinds of root medicine and the black dyed cloth called *iyaji* (in fact it was more a navy blue but to the Ibos, who loved things colourful, bright and flowery, anything dark-ish and plain was black). Even the Northerners — the Hausas, and the tall, graceful Fulani shepherds with their leather knapsacks, leather slippers, long whitish robes and dark brown turbans — had stalls. Some of their families had settled permanently in the houses along Otu market and sold delicious Hausa dishes, such as corn and bean dumplings laced with roasted meat in honey, and the beef known as *efi Awusa*. Their women had large holes in their ears through which they wedged bright coral beads bought with the money they made buying and selling in Ibo towns.

People pushed and jostled, hawkers added to the din, and in general everyone seemed to have a great deal to say. Ojebeta, though frightened and clutching Okolie, found it fascinating. So many people and so many different kinds of Ibo dialect! Her hold on her brother became tighter as she began to notice that people were staring at her. She felt humiliated when she saw a group of women with trays of cassava pulp on their heads laughing and pointing in her direction; one of them, trying to be modest, was looking away to hide her laughter.

Ojebeta glanced at her brother, then down at herself, and asked, "Why are they staring at me so, and laughing?"

Okolie was finding it hard to control his nagging guilt, and as he guided her through the noisy crowds — through the stalls of the fish sellers and the yam sellers, towards a more open space in the market — he did not at first hear her question. He heard eventually, after she had tugged him and shouted louder; he knew, however, that to give her a full explanation would take long minutes, so he patted her shoulder as if to say she should not worry about those silly people who had nothing better to do than stand there laughing like people with broken heads.

He knew why they were laughing. It was not just because of Ojebeta's safety charms, the bells and cowrie shells that jingled and clanged when she made the slightest movement. It was because his sister also had a very interesting face. All over her features were traced intricate tattoos, the pattern of spinach leaves, with delicate branches running down the bridge of her nose, spreading out on her forehead and ending up at the top of her ears. On each cheek was drawn the outline of a large spinach leaf looking ready to be picked. It was not that many Ibos did not have facial tribal marks of different kinds, rather that a few would have put so many on the face of one little girl. But Ojebeta's mother Umeadi, when she realised that her daughter was going to live, had had a reason for going to the expense of engaging the services of the most costly face-marker in Ibuza. For, with such a riot of tribal spinach marks on her only daughter's face, no kidnapper would dream of selling her into slavery. What was more, if she got lost her people would always know her, for although the patterns on her face might seem madness here to these Ibos from the East who frequented Otu Onitsha market, among the Western Ibos called the Aniochas it was a distinctive and meaningful design.

The thought of cutting off Ojebeta's charms occurred to her brother Okolie. Among her own people they were not such a strange affair, but they were out of place in the middle of one of the largest markets in West Africa. They were supposed to be for domestic purposes. Usually it was thought safe to remove such charms from a child when that child could talk coherently enough for any living adult to understand, so that if her persecutors from the other world should ask her to come with them, she could shout, "Go away, I don't want you. I am happy here." Then the adult could take a broom or whatever and start to beat all the corners of the room saying, "Asha, asha," until the child stopped calling for help. For most children this age for removing their safety charms was when they were about four or five years old; they were then regarded as having walked out of childhood and become members of the living world.

But Ogbanje Ojebeta was dearer to her mother than that. She had wanted to make assurance doubly sure, and had allowed her daughter to carry the charms for so long as insurance that she would survive. It was almost as if her mother, without meaning to, had wanted to keep Ojebeta a baby as long as possible, since no little brother or sister followed her. Now Okolie was too frightened of the possible consequences to risk removing the bells and cowries himself.

45

"Suppose anything should happen to her," he thought. "They would say that I killed her. No, let her wear them until I get her into the house of a master."

Moreover, who could tell what trick their dead parents might be contriving now they were both on the other side? They might be longing to have their only daughter with them and might frighten her to death in her sleep. Who could foretell the thoughts of the dead, even if they were our loved ones? He believed that the living should belong to the living. Ojebeta should be given every opportunity to live her own life, and die in peace when her time came. Not be pulled along by their parents who now belonged to the dead, before she was even able to tell what life looked like.

Their last push and jostle through the crowd round those selling fresh meat brought Okolie and Ojebeta to some stalls that looked very clean and elegant and less noisy. It was as if the women of these stalls were of a different breed, well dressed like people having a special outing. At many of the stalls there were very young girls sitting on low stools with heads bowed, doing some kind of sewing. Ojebeta watched avidly as they passed these colourful stalls of the cloth sellers. They halted rather abruptly in front of one of them, and she guessed that they had reached their destination.

It was a strange destination for a child of seven. She could not have imagined in her most wild dream that this was where they were going. They had walked for miles and for hours and through various kinds of forests, waded streams and been ferried in a canoe to come this far. And now they stood before this gaily coloured stall where thousands of cloths of different patterns hung in rows on wooden shelves. There were so many colours and designs that they all seemed to merge into each other. Some had patterns of leaves on them, some had birds, some fish, some had a design like the mortar used to pound yam — whatever object you could think of, there was bound to be an agbada material that had that design.

Sitting on a long bench on the floor were four young girls, aged between nine and fourteen. They were all dressed identically in material with a pattern of cowries on it: the background of the cloth was white and the cowries were deep blue shapes with their edges tinged in yellow. Ojebeta noticed these details only on a closer look, for at first the cloth just looked bluish. They had stopped in front of one of these girls.

"Where is your mother?" Okolie asked in a low, dry voice.

Two girls looked up, and one of the younger ones gave a con-

46

spiratorial nudge to the largest and apparently the eldest girl. The latter looked up from her sewing and covered her mouth to prevent the laugh that wanted to escape at the sight of this queer looking pair at their stall. She could tell from their clothes and from their tribal markings, particularly those on the little girl's face, that they were not from the bush interior but from the Aniocha area. But they certainly were an odd pair, with this big healthy man, in his prime of youth, walking up to stalls in Otu and asking people, "Where is your mother?" without any form of greeting.

"Look," whispered the smallest girl, loudly enough for Okolie and Ojebeta to hear, "look, she is wearing bells like market dancers."

The big girl, who had by now composed herself again, told the small girl to keep quiet and keep her eyes on her work or she would take her to Pa Palagada when they got home. At the mention of that name there was such an unnatural hush that one would have thought that whoever this person or apparition called "Pa Palagada" was his powers must be immense. Peace suddenly descended; even the girl sniggering and pointing at nothing bent her neck and glued her eyes to her sewing.

The big girl seemed to think Okolie wished to buy some abada material for Ojebeta, for she took out the wooden measure and waited for him to tell her which he wanted of the innumerable cloths supplied to them mainly by the United Africa Company Europeans.

Okolie studied her with interest. She was an attractive grown girl of about fourteen with large breasts. She looked well fed and so fresh and plump that her skin reminded him of smooth, ripe mangoes, ready to burst open oozing out rich, creamy, sugary juice. He wondered why Ibuza girls were not like that; they were usually thin, with long legs and narrow faces. Well, he debated within himself, this girl probably sat here all day and maybe the most work she did was to fetch firewood for the family or pound yam for the evening meal. An Ibuza girl of her age would have to help her mother plant cassava, help her father peel corn from the cobs when they were ripe, and on her way back from the farm she would carry heads of ripe palm kernels ready to be pressed into oil which could be sold here in the Otu market, apart from that oil kept for the family's cooking and oil lamps. But these girls in Otu did not have to lead such itinerant lives. Although some of them were in fact slaves — Ma Palagada would have paid a sum on their heads, just as he was expecting her to pay something for his sister Ojebeta

47

— yet they appeared to be treated just like the children in any family.

This strengthened his belief that he was doing the right thing for Ojebeta. He was sure Ma Palagada would treat her like one of these girls under her care. He imagined his sister in one of the outfits the girls were wearing; in Ibuza she could only dress like that for big important days, whereas here the girls were well turned out for the Otu market. He also liked their way of speaking the Ibo language, with a tinge of foreign sophistication, not the brash, harsh and pointed accents of his own people who because they were people of the interior did not have to live and trade with as many foreigners as these Ibos of Otu Onitsha. Many Ibo traders came from wherever their homes were just to make money at the Otu market, so that they could buy lands, build fine modern Victorian houses and live very modern, clean and foreign lives.

The big girl went on to say, like someone chanting, that they had just had a brand new supply of abada from the coast.

"You see this one — we call it 'Ejekom be loya' ('I have a date with a lawyer')," she sang, pointing with the long wooden measure to a cloth with a plain white background and a border of yellow, pale blue and pink. "You can't get this from any other stall here in Otu market. Our Ma Palagada has bought the sole right to it for the next four markets from those white U.A.C. people. So if you buy it now for yourself and a yard or two for your girl-wife, you will both be in the height of fashion. People will never stop looking at you and admiring you both because they will never have seen a cloth so smooth and beautiful as this. It looks very like the white otuogwu your people like to wear. Just feel its smoothness. It is a cloth in a million." Then she paused, both for breath and to assure herself that she had been saying the right thing.

Okolie had to smile. His red lips parted uncontrollably, and he had to steel himself so as not to burst out into a roaring type of laughter. He wiped away the tears of amusement that had sprung into his eyes, and said:

"All right, now you listen to me for a while. Did I tell you that I have come here to buy cloth? I asked of your mother, but you have not answered me. The cloth is fine, well designed, but I did not come here to buy cloth. I have come to have a word with your mother. Where is she?"

Okolie's voice had so much authority and impatience in it that all three girls sitting looked up at him, and the big girl who had

48

been trying to make an impression simply gaped. People did not come to the market asking for Ma Palagada just like that, particularly not this type of person, even though his voice was commanding.

"She is not at the stall," she said curtly. "Do you want me to leave a message? I shall give it to her when she returns." She turned round as if to resume her needlework and forget everything about this insolent farmer who came to the Otu market from God-knows-where to be so audacious.

But Okolie's voice cut her short. He stepped right into the shed that formed the stall. The other girls held their breath, ready to let out a scream just in case they were going to be attacked by a market thief in broad daylight. They had all heard stories from other stalls where there were usually crowds about thieves who would move in on the seller, shouting for her attendance while other members of the gang were making away with goods meant for sale; that was mostly at the stalls of the dry fish sellers, not in the section of those selling cloth. You might also be given counterfeit paper money or even coins minted by some clever persons; but few thieves would think of coming this way and dragging a little girl with cowrie charms and spinach face along. The girls were alarmed, and puzzled, though without losing their outward composure.

"Get out of the stall," said the big girl menacingly, holding on fast to the wooden measure, "or I will call the market police."

Okolie ignored her and sat down in a space at the edge of the bench. "I have a special message for your mother," he announced. "I have come all the way from Ibuza to give her the message. I am a relative of hers. That is why I have come, not to steal cloth. Steal my relative's cloth? Tah! I would never do a thing like that. And this is my sister, not my wife."

This latest statement intensified the laughter which had been bubbling within the girls, who were not very keen on their sewing anyway. First, they found it difficult to see any kind of resemblance between Ma Palagada and this farmer; the fact too that the big girl could have imagined the man's little sister was his wife made them laugh the more.

"Don't blame me," said the big girl, defending herself. "The Owerri people marry their wives like that, and then come to the market for her to be equipped."

Okolie nodded. "Not just Owerri people. Many of our people do it." To himself he said, *Is it not almost the same as I am now about*

49

to do to my little sister, young as she is — marry her away to this woman relative? So why condemn the Owerri people or anyone else who does that kind of thing.

As a gesture of affection, and to help assuage his guilt, he pulled Ogbanje Ojebeta on to his lap and they sat there on the bench, watching the bustle and jostle of the market. He wondered why God had created so many people, and for what reason. And why some of the people created could be as rich as this Ma Palagada and her husband and others as poor as those in Ibuza where he came from, so many farmers all struggling for survival. Then the thought occurred to him that after his Uloko dance he could consider becoming a trader himself. After all, he was going to get some money from Ma Palagada today. His imaginings were not disappointed as he watched the number of customers who came to the stall to buy yards and yards of cloth. One or two even bought the handkerchiefs which the girls were making from scraps of material. The big girl mended some torn cloths for a few people; and all the time the customers paid money, all money. Yes, he was going to get so much money for his sister.

He drew the tired little girl Ojebeta closer to him, and she put her head on his broad shoulder, trusting him as any sister would trust her brother, her only visible relative.

5 A Necessary Evil

It was now past midday, and it was still very hot. The sun was shifting from the centre of the sky to one side. Okolie was thankful that when they had met Eze at Asaba he had at least given Ojebeta some food. She yawned and stretched like a tired cat, and he kept assuring her that their relatives would soon come. Thirsty, Okolie asked the girls for some water. One of them went to fetch a big green bottle which they kept under one of the benches away from the sun and poured some water into a white bowl with a blue rim for him to drink. He admired the smoothness of the bowl, rubbing his rough farm fingers all over it, then gulped down the cool liquid and asked for more. The girls started to giggle again; these girls laughed at everything, he thought. He could not, however, finish the second bowl so he gave the rest of the water to his sister.

Ojebeta noticed that the water here tasted different, as if something had been added to it. She was about to ask her brother about it when they heard a group of laughing female voices approaching. One of the girls called in a voice so low, so urgent and so sibilantly formed that Ojebeta thought something terrible must be about to happen:

"Chiago, Nwayinuzo — shh . . . shh. . . . They are coming. They are coming. . . ."

At once heads were once more bent to work. The big girl called Chiago stood with the wooden cloth measure in her hand like a soldier on guard, almost behind Okolie and his sister. The owners of the jocular voices were still hidden by a stall that jutted into the middle of the passageway. Many other people came and went. Ojebeta was silent in expectation. Okolie's stomach started to rumble in apprehension.

They heard the leave-takings and farewells; and then a very big lady appeared from around the corner — a lady who was tall of

51

bearing, a lady who was very proud. She had a large, very sensuous mouth, and the laughter was still on her lips. She was also the most well dressed person Ojebeta had ever seen. She was wearing a brown abada with fish patterns on it, a yellow blouse, and silk scarf on her head. She walked with easy steps, saying hello to this stall and how-do-you-do to that person. She seemed to know everybody and they responded to her warmth.

"There she is," said Chiago unnecessarily under her breath, while keeping a straight face and not looking in the direction of the woman who was their owner.

At last Ma Palagada strolled into her stall and greeted them fulsomely.

"Oh, oh — have you been waiting for me long? Why did you not tell the girls to come for me? I was at a meeting with the U.A.C. people. Welcome! Welcome! Have they given you something to eat? Is this the little sister you talked about? Welcome. Oh, my! She is just a baby. For her to have lost everyone. . . . Still, God knows best. Welcome!"

A velveteen cushion on a bench was plumped up for her to sit on. Okolie watched and answered her in monosyllables, indicating that, no, they had not eaten anything: the girls had not known who he was.

At this Ma Palagada laughed; it was not a very loud sound but it had a mellow richness in it. It was the laughter of the well fed, the laughter of someone who had not known for a very long time what it was to be hungry. "We shall soon take care of that. These thoughtless girls should have given you something."

She looked down again at Ojebeta, appraising her from head to foot, then called her to come to her.

Ojebeta did not want to go and she clung to her brother. It was not that she did not like her relative but that the whole show was just too sudden for the poor child. What did this woman want with her? She might be a relative, but Ojebeta had never seen her before; moreover, she did not look like any relative she had ever seen before. All this cloth on her stall and the amount she had on herself, and her way of speaking the Ibo language — Ojebeta was overwhelmed. No, she did not want to go to her.

It was at this point that she had the first clue of what was in store for her, for here something like suppressed anger escaped from her brother. His voice was direct and businesslike, almost as if he were someone who did not know who she was, a stranger to

52

her. Ojebeta was so startled that she burst into tears and called out: "My mother, please come to me. I am lost!"

Ma Palagada was moved and told Okolie to be gentle with his sister. "Come," she urged Ojebeta, "I only want to greet you. You haven't even said a single word to me. Come. I am your relative, you know. Come. You mustn't be frightened of us. We are not bad people. Just come here. . . ."

Okolie pulled and half carried Ojebeta to the lady who, with a smile on her face, felt her arms and peered into her eyes, then smiled again and asked, "Are you hungry?"

Ojebeta was a child brought up with so much love and so much trust that it never occurred to her to distrust a smiling face. Her tears had been a reaction to this new voice she heard her brother whom she had known all her life use to her; now the voice had stopped. She nodded her head vigorously up and down like a mad lizard. Yes, of course she was hungry.

She heard the other girls giggling again. Now what had she done? Ojebeta wondered in bewilderment, hating the smallest girl who sniggered the most. She felt like fighting that girl, for she was not much bigger than herself, but she ignored her and kept on nodding.

"You shall have some food," Ma Palagada said. "Chiago, go to the food stalls and buy Ogbanje — is that your name? — buy her a piece of agidi from those people from Accra. Have you eaten their agidi before? It is very nice."

Ojebeta nodded once more; she had tasted "agidi Akala", as her dead mother used to call it. On the days her mother used to go to Onitsha she would buy one large piece, and Ojebeta and all her friends and her father would sit up and wait for her to come home from Otu, just to have their little bits of Accra agidi. In those days it had been a real delicacy for her; and now she was once more going to have some to eat, her mouth watered like a dog's. Ma Palagada gave some money to the big girl Chiago, who ran among the other stalls, turned a corner and disappeared into the market. They all waited. More customers came. Okolie and Ma Palagada talked blatant nothings to gain time. Sitting away from her brother, apart from the other girls, Ojebeta thought of her mother, her father, of the "agidi Akala" she was going to have.

Chiago soon arrived with the corn dough steaming. It was the first time Ojebeta had seen it hot, for the agidi her mother used to buy was always cold by the time she reached home from the market. She watched Chiago peeling the wrapping leaves off and putting

53

them into another white bowl.

"Do you want pepper on it?" asked Chiago then.

Ma Palagada, who had seemed to be unaware of the goings on, intervened: "Let her do it the way she wants. Give her the pepper and salt. She can spice it herself."

So Chiago handed Ojebeta the whitest and the best agidi she had ever seen in her life. At first Ojebeta did not know what to do. Should she eat it all, or share it with the others, her brother in particular?

Okolie saw her dilemma and said, with his mouth watering, "Eat it, it's all for you."

Ojebeta could not believe her ears. The other girls did not even look as if they were at all interested. Why, in her home five people would have shared this, for agidi was regarded as something special, not heavy enough to be everyday food. She did the only thing that she felt was right: she scooped one big handful and gave it to her brother. The latter looked this way and that way, felt ashamed and said with little heart:

"No, my sister, you eat it. Your relative bought it for you."

That was strange, thought Ojebeta. But if Okolie had gone off his food, what of the new relative she had just acquired, who had been kind enough to buy all this hot agidi with fresh pepper and salt? She walked up to her with the innocence of a child who had never been taught to fear adults and said, "Have some, it's nice." Ma Palagada smiled, called her a good little girl but said that she had eaten; they had had their midday meal before she went to the meeting. So Ojebeta could eat it all. She hurried back to the bench and, sitting with her head bent to one side, busied herself with her day's good luck — a whole piece of agidi Akala to herself.

Ma Palagada and Okolie talked and talked in voices so low that Ojebeta did not bother to make any attempt to find out what they were saying. It was too much of an effort, and besides what did it matter at the moment. So immersed was she in the agidi that she scarcely heard her brother announce:

"I am going to the food stalls to eat some pounded yam. I shall not be long."

Ojebeta looked up and nodded.

"I will show you the way," Ma Palagada said casually to Okolie. "Chiago, take care of the stall. I shall not be long."

"Yes, Ma," said Chiago.

Ojebeta went on scooping the agidi into her mouth, showing it off

54

as she did so to the youngest girl, whom she had heard them refer to as Amanna. But Amanna did not even seem to envy her, and instead laughed each time Ojebeta scooped the food up. The urge to fight this cheeky girl was becoming strong, though once more she managed to ignore her while polishing the bowl with her fingers, at the same time making a great deal of noise with her mouth. It had been a delicious meal and Ojebeta was now full; though the last bit had been cold and not as tasty as when she first started it, she finished it all.

Now she looked about her, pleased with the world. The other girls still giggled, but she had decided to take no notice of their foolish behaviour. She sat perched on the wooden bench by the edge of the stall so that she would be the first to catch a glimpse of her brother and Ma Palagada when they showed up eventually. She watched people come in and out of the stall and was fascinated by the fast method the girl Chiago used to mend torn clothes, for she had never before seen a sewing machine. She wished she too could have a go at the black monster with yellow patterns on it. When Chiago wound it, it made sounds as if it was singing, and after it sang on each piece of cloth they came out stitched together so well and so quickly. This way, she noticed, it was not necessary to use needles like her mother had used for sewing tears in her cloth.

After Ojebeta had watched this for a while, the longing for her brother and for them to be going home from the market began to increase. She could see that some other people were already starting to leave. Yet Ma Palagada's girls sat there, doing their sewing, intermittently singing scraps of song, but looking as if they were willing to wait the whole day if necessary. Ojebeta was fed up of waiting. The sweet sensation the hot agidi had given her was fast evaporating and giving way to a kind of boredom, tinged somewhat with rebellion. Not wanting to ask the permission of these unfriendly strangers, she scrambled up from her seat, determined to go and find her brother. Had he not promised Uteh's husband that they would be back home before the evening meal? Well, it was fast approaching sundown and she knew they had a very long trek ahead of them. She then realised how tired her feet were, but the urge to go home was far more pressing than her need to give in to fatigue.

As she took a few steps from the stall, the girls looked at her and all of a sudden stopped their endless chatter. Chiago was the first to find her tongue.

"Where are you going, little girl from Ibuza?"

55

"I am going to look for my brother," came the unpolished reply. For once the other girls did not laugh at her. Only Amanna made a slight tittering sound but was quickly hushed by Chiago's stern glance. The latter was thinking fast to herself: *Poor parentless child. They probably did not tell her. She probably does not know she may never see her brother again. Poor girl.*

Aloud she said, not without pity, "Come back, little Ibuza girl. Your big brother will soon be here. Come back, or you will get lost in the market, and the child-catchers from the coast will take you away in their canoes. Come back."

Ojebeta stood and looked at her for a moment, wondering why the child-catchers should want to take her away. She had, it was true, heard stories of people going missing even in Ibuza, but that such a fate could befall her was beyond belief. After all, she was only going to get her brother, over there round the corner. She would run faster than any child-catcher in the world, and once she had found her big brother Okolie who would dare catch her?

"Will my 'little father' be here soon?" she asked, seeking further reassurance.

"Of course he will. What have we been telling you?" replied Chiago, her eyes averted.

Ojebeta did not know what came over her then, except that it was connected with her having been brought up by simple people who looked you straight in the eye because they had nothing to hide. The way this big girl spoke to her, the way the others all at once seemed to be made of mechanical wood, working without feeling at their work and not daring to look at her, made her uneasy. She did not want to wait to find out what they were being so cagey about; all she wanted was her brother and for them both to go back home to Ibuza, where her aunt Uteh would be waiting for her with pounded yam and palm soup and little crabs from the Oboshi stream. All the girls were seemingly engrossed in their sewing, and she told herself that they were not watching her. She knew where her brother Okolie was — just round the corner, at the stalls of the food sellers. If she ran that way she would surely find him, still sitting there eating yam and stew. She would find him, before these girls ever caught up with her. She would find him. . . .

And just like a hunter's arrow that had been quivering impatiently in its bow while the hunter covered his prey until the opportune moment to let fly, so did Ogbanje Ojebeta dash out of the Palagada cloth stall. She ran, almost flew like an arrow, her little legs like wings, her heart beating fast in fear and anticipation, going as she thought to her brother — her brother, the only person she knew in this market full of strange people, the only person who would take her home to their town, the only person who had brought her here. She made music with her metal charms and cowries as she ran to meet him. She was an unusual sight among the sophisticated, rich, fat mammy traders who formed the backbone of Onitsha market.

"If I can't find him, my big brother," she said to herself as she ran, "I shall go back to Ibuza to the hut of my big mother and wait for him."

But it was to be an abortive attempt at freedom.

At the end of the line of cloth stalls was a very big one belonging to a fat mammy called Ma Mee, who was one of the richest Onitsha marketwomen at the time. She, like Ma Palagada, had a double stall, but her twin stalls curved into the pathway, almost blocking the way from the riverside. Hers was a corner site, and the fact that she occupied this privileged position had been the cause of a great deal of backbiting and bickering among the other cloth traders, particularly the smaller fry who had only a single stall. They said that it was because of Ma Mee's advantageous placing that she sold more cloth than the rest of them put together. They said that her situation made it possible for her to see prospective buyers coming up from the canoes; they said that very few customers passed through her stalls without buying anything. But, as often happens in like circumstances, no one could bring themselves to tell her to her face. Ma Mee had been in the selling business for a long time. She knew that people talked among themselves, for from time to time some of the hurtful things others said about her did reach her ears. But she reasoned to herself, "If I go about challenging all the things people say about me, who will be my friend? For whoever I challenge about spiteful things they are said to have said about me, that person will deny it, and I will only have added one more enemy to the list I already have." So she behaved as if the gossip did not exist, and this spirit endeared her to many other traders who consequently came to regard her as having great maturity. In fact in avoiding the trouble of having open enemies, she was simply being prudent, for there were occasions when each trader needed the goodwill of the others, for example when robbers — well aware that the cloth stalls contained valuable materials and belonged mainly to a few wealthy and privileged women — would organise themselves for raids. But if one stall could raise the alarm and the thief was seen,

God have mercy on his soul. These were women who did not have time for the police; they could not afford to lose a day's trade by going to a court or going to see a chief. They invariably dealt with the culprit in the way they themselves thought fit.

The same fate awaited any runaway domestic slave. Many of the market women had slaves in great number to help them with the fetching and carrying that went with being a full-time trader — and also in the vain hope that one day the British people at the coast would go and some of these house slaves could be sold abroad, just as their fathers and grandfathers had done, so profitably that the abundance of capital and property they had built could still be seen in many families round Onitsha and Bonny and Port Harcourt.

On this hot afternoon, a tiresome and very hungry Ibo beggar of a fisherman had caught a sizeable thorn fish which he had brought to the prosperous cloth sellers. He had expected to sell it at a higher price than Ma Mee was offering, and because he was anxious for the extra money to take home to the hinterland to feed his needy family he stayed on and was haggling and haggling. Ma Mee was really beginning to pity him and the unfortunate fish that was still alive, wriggling its body and fighting desperately for air. Although its protective thorns could be deadly to an enemy and were all spread out in its fruitless struggle to free itself, the fisherman did not want to kill it outright for he could show prospective buyers that it had just been caught and, better than just fresh, was still alive. The fisherman became more despondent as Ma Mee would not agree to the price he wanted and as he saw that the fish's resistance was growing more feeble, whether because it now realised it was fighting a losing battle or because of the effects of having been out of the water for so long on such a hot afternoon. He stopped dangling the fish on the powerful wire which he had strung through its open mouth, and was summoning up the courage to touch its slimy body, at the same time as Ma Mee was beginning to feel compelled to buy it from him, when they all — the fisherman, Ma Mee and the girl slaves who had been passive throughout the preceding argument — heard the cries of alarm of the girls at Ma Palagada's stalls.

Everyone's first involuntary reaction was to look for a club, a knife, even the wooden measuring stick, to arm themselves with ready to fight to protect their own territory, as it were. They all dashed out, led by the poor fisherman who wanted to play the role of a gallant man preserving the women from robbers.

Ma Mee was a big woman, so big that she never stopped perspiring. But there were certain happenings which appeared to make her weightless: happenings such as market thieves and runaways. For if you did not help your neighbour in such a situation, the day the same trouble befell you, people would turn a blind eye rather than offer assistance; it was an unwritten law among the traders on the banks of the Niger. So, tightening her voluminous lappa round her substantial posterior, her breasts heaving in unison to her great haste, she rushed forward prepared to do battle with and if necessary maim this market thief causing the outcry, if she could lay hands on whoever it was, for daring to go into her absent colleague's stall.

However, it was not a market thief that they saw; it was a sight so peculiar that people simply stared bemused as it sped past their stalls — Chiago tearing along the pathway chasing a small, helpless and terrified child: a little girl festooned with bells and cowrie shells, just like a slave prepared for sacrifice! They stared, and did not understand.

Chiago's cries soon put them in the picture.

"Hold her! Please hold her for me, she is new — hold her!"

But she did not look at all like any slave girl Ma Mee had ever seen before, this little creature who more or less ran into her arms for protection and cried out:

"Oh, my mother, I am lost."

For a split second, Ma Mee held her, as she would have embraced her very own child; then she let go of the fugitive but still barred her way with her great bulk.

"You are not lost, little girl with pagan charms," she replied. "You are just a domestic slave."

Almost fainting with that kind of disappointment and sense of unfairness which is sometimes inexplicable, Ojebeta the only living daughter of Umeadi cried out once more in despair, this time to her dead mother:

"Save me, Mother, for now I am lost."

Unable to go forward past Ma Mee, she had no alternative but to allow herself to be caught by her pursuer.

"Let me go, let me go!" Ojebeta screamed as she wriggled violently in the hands of Chiago, the biggest of the Palagada girls.

Chiago would have held Ojebeta gently except that she knew it was likely to have resulted in real trouble for herself. So she gripped

59

her tightly, masking her pity for this parentless child by explaining unnecessarily to the crowd, and especially to Ma Mee, that Ojebeta had only just arrived that very afternoon.

Ma Mee did not envy her neighbour for having four girl slaves; and this new little one would bring the total number of Palagada slaves to seven, since they also had two male slaves who had been bought or captured — she was not quite sure of the story — from among the people called the Urhobos. It was said that Pa Palagada had bought the men from some Potokis who were leaving the country and returning to their own land. The two, who were young boys at the time, could not remember where they had originally come from, so they were given Ibo names and were put to work on the Palagada farms. Sometimes Ma Palagada would bring to the Otu market the big yams that these two hardworking and now hefty men had produced. So as far as Ma Mee was concerned the Palagadas already had as many slaves as they needed; after all, one couldn't sell them abroad as in the old days. However, she kept all these thoughts to herself.

Chiago thanked Ma Mee in the way she had been taught to greet important ladies like her, with a curtsy, and half pulled, half carried Ojebeta back to their own stall, knowing that the eyes of all the other women were following her. As she tried to lessen the shock for the poor girl, Chiago too was near tears, remembering how it had come about that she herself had been sold.

That year had been a bad one for her family. Where exactly her village was to be found was now shrouded in obscurity, though she knew she came from somewhere not far from the rivers where Pa Palagada went to sell palm kernels to some foreigners near Bonny. But she could remember that she had had a mother who was forever bearing children, and who was always carrying a baby on her back, held there with a tiny piece of cloth which was all she had. Then came a year when the rains were so heavy that almost all the vegetation, except the oil palms, was carried away. Her father had brought her to this dark bearded, overblown and formidable-looking man, who told her that his daughter was getting married just like the white people did. Her father told her that they needed a little girl to wear white muslin and to carry flowers for this man's beautiful daughter. Having done that service, she would be well paid, and her father would be waiting for her by the river, with the very canoe with which they had come. She had believed her father, especially when it was explained to her that the money

60

she would earn would be used to pay the native doctors who would make her mother well again. And then their life would be back to normal. They would live in their house on the boat, and come to land to sell the fish they caught, and when it became too wet to live on the water, they would come to land and plant and eat cocoyam, *ede*, and sometimes yam. . . .

Chiago remembered that she had had to cross another river, and they had walked what seemed endless numbers of miles. For days they had walked and they were so tired that for part of the journey Pa Palagada had to be carried by local bearers in a hammock. At a town called Arochukwu they had stayed for days, and it was here that she had a bitter taste of what life held in store for her. She did not see the so-called daughter of Pa Palagada; in fact she seldom saw him at all. She was thrust into a small room at the back of the house with other strange people, who all seemed unhappy and, like her, scantily dressed. They all ate together, and had to go to the stream to fetch water, and she had to help in the large cooking place they called the "kinsheni", or something like that. She had stayed there with Pa Palagada and his entourage for just five days, and then they had set off again walking and walking and only resting at occasional drinking and eating places. They crossed another fairly small river in a canoe, and by this time Chiago had not even been able to remember from which direction she had originally come.

She had thought about it constantly since, and had finally decided that she had no choice but to accept things as they were. Her family would certainly have starved had she not been sold to this man, Pa Palagada, who had later handed Chiago to his wife. It was a blessing that at least her stomach had been sold with her, so her parents would no longer have to worry about how to feed her; and perhaps the money her head had fetched had helped her family for a while.

The picture of her family, however, had dimmed after eleven years with her mistress and her husband. The long stay had taught her a great many things. The most important was that a slave who made an unsuccessful attempt to run away was better off dead. Such a slave would be so tortured that he or she would be useless as a person, or else might be used for burial.

She had watched one such horrible burial when she had been about twelve and was travelling with Ma Palagada in the Ibo interior. The chief wife of the master of the house had died, and it was necessary for her husband to send her to the land of the dead accompanied by a female slave. The one chosen was a particularly beautiful slave, with smooth skin and black closely cropped hair, who was said to be a princess captured in war from another Ibo village; she had made attempts to return to where she came from, but unfortunately her new owner caught her and she lost her freedom of movement. On the eve of the burial she was brought and ordered to lie down in the shallow grave. As might be expected, she resisted, but there was no pity on the faces of the men who stood by watching, amused by her cries. She made appeals to the gods of her people to save her, she begged some of the mourners to spare her life, saying that her father the chief of another village would repay them, but to no avail. One of the sons of the dead woman lost his patience and, maybe out of mercy and a wish to have it all done with as quickly as possible, took a club and struck the defenceless woman hard at the back of her shaved head. The more Chiago thought about it in later years, the more convinced she was that the woman slave must have had seven lives. She did not drop down into the grave she was later to share with her dead mistress as was then expected. Instead she turned to look at the chief, who was calling on his son to cease his brutality, and she said to him, "For showing me this little mercy, chief, I shall come again, I shall come again. . . ."

She was not allowed to finish her valedictory statement, for the stubborn young man, disregarding his father's appeal, gave the woman a final blow so that she fell by the side of the grave. But she was still struggling even when the body of her dead mistress was placed on her. She still fought and cried out, so alive. Soon her voice was completely silenced by the damp earth that was piled on both her and the dead woman.

Chiago never quite recovered from this early shock, not even when sometime later she heard Ma Palagada talking to another woman trader about it and ending up by saying that one of the chief's younger wives now had a baby daughter very like the slave princess who had been buried alive; to clinch the resemblance, this little girl was born with a lump on the back of her head, in the same place as where the slave princess had been struck. . . .

Chiago had seen, too, many slaves who had become successful, who had worked so well with their masters that they themselves became wealthy traders at Otu market, given their freedom when their masters grew old. The majority of them, particularly the male slaves, did not wish to go home, if they could even remember which part of the country they had come from originally. Some of them stayed because they could not return to their region as a result of some atrocity they had committed. One of the Palagada slaves was born a twin and her people, somewhere among the Efiks, did not accept twins; her mother had nursed her secretly and later had her sold, simply to give her a chance in life.

If only Chiago could have communicated all that passed through her mind to this struggling little girl. She wished she could tell her that the only course left for her was to make the best of everything, by being docile and trouble-free. She had stopped holding her too tightly but had her arms round the girl's naked waist, looking at her with pity as if she were her own sister. In fact they would soon be like sisters — did not the same fate await them?

"I shall tell my father of you," Ojebeta whimpered in between exhausted hiccoughs. In her confusion after the long, wearying journey and her escape attempt, she imagined her father was still alive and well in Ibuza. She stared at everyone in front of the stalls they passed, hoping that one of them would be her brother.

If the girls felt like reminding Ojebeta that her parents were long dead, they restrained themselves. They had seen scenes like this played out before their very eyes too often, and they knew from experience that to indulge in a little fantasy would do her no harm at all; if anything, it would do her good. So they let her wallow in her own world of wishful thinking. She went on repeating that she would tell her father, her mother and her big mother Uteh, until she was completely exhausted.

Ma Mee soon strolled round to their stall to find out how they were coping and whether Ma Palagada was back. Chiago replied that she was sure she would be back soon, and this statement awakened in Ojebeta a last, futile hope to gain sympathy.

"Please, kind mother, can you bring my brother back for me? He only went there round your stall to eat pounded yam."

"Yes," Ma Mee replied in a soft voice, "I shall bring your brother back. But do you want me to buy you anything to eat? Do you want honeyed meat balls from the Hausa people down the coast?"

Ojebeta shook her head vigorously as though she would snap it off from her body. She did not want anything, not anymore, not from these people who had tricked her into letting Okolie out of her sight because of some hot agidi.

"I don't want anything. I only want to go home." She little realised in what circumstances and how long it would be before that going home took place.

Ma Mee walked back to her stall telling herself that buying and selling people could not be helped. "Where would we be without slave labour, and where would some of these unwanted children be without us?" It might be evil, but it was a necessary evil.

6 Lost Identity

Ma Palagada heaved a sigh of relief when it was all over — the haggling and arguing over a few pounds. She was perfectly satisfied with the world, happy at her own luck and was looking forward to returning to her own stalls, collecting her human purchase and going home. The sun was fast going down, the gentle wind from the river was becoming stronger and she was getting tired and hungry for a properly cooked meal, not the over-spiced stuff from the market stalls.

As she jostled and pushed her way among the noisy crowd, she went through the day's business in her mind. She smiled as she congratulated herself on her bargaining tactics. She had given Okolie exactly eight English pounds for his sister; but what a long time both of them had taken to admit acceptance. She knew that he needed the money, that he could not look after his sister and did not want his aunt Uteh to take her. Ma Palagada also knew that Okolie was hungry and, since a hungry man was an angry man, that was the first thing to rectify.

She had ordered from the best pounded yam stall in Otu market, and it was served piping hot, with the aroma from the kelenkele soup curling visibly in the form of a dewy steam. Okolie swallowed emptily so much at the sight of the food that he seemed in danger of consuming his own tongue. She did not stop at food, but asked the young girl serving there to bring him a small keg of undiluted palm wine. Not waiting to be invited twice Okolie had pounced on the food. Ma Palagada reminded him after his first gulped mouthful that the water in the calabash bowl was for washing his hands.

"The dirt on my hand is from my body, the good food is going into my body," he replied, "what do I need to wash for, eh?"

She had smiled gently but said no more. Watching him eat, she saw that his hands were black to the nails, the typical hands of a

65

farmer. The fingers were permanently curved and she had wondered why this was in so young a person. Perhaps it was due to the way he cut the pounded yam — scooping a piece of it in his curved fingers, rolling it into a nice lump, rolling it again in the soup, and then scooping it up, soup and all, into his ever-opened mouth and swallowing, his throat going *gbim, gbim.*

For the first five minutes while Okolie was busy doing all this and eyeing the big chunks of bush meat, his whole being was aware of nothing but the food and his good fortune in having been given such a great deal to eat. The meat and the soup with its ingredients would have been enough to fill a whole family of ten at home; he was beginning to see that with people like Ma Palagada meat was not just a delicacy one tasted on feast days or on the few occasions when a member of one's family had caught a bush pig in a trap but a big meal on its own. After he had been eating for a while, and had paused to sample the palm wine, he addressed Ma Palagada.

"Have you eaten? Why don't you join me?"

Her big chest rippled with barely suppressed amusement. *Your little sister had the courtesy to offer her agidi to others before she even tasted it herself, but you, her big brother, made sure you were half filled before inviting me, who bought it for you,* she thought with disgust at the man.

"No, my relative," she told him, disguising her feelings. "You get on with the job of eating the food. It is for you that I bought it. I had mine earlier on. This one is for you."

The relief in Okolie's eyes was very clear. It had been a half-hearted invitation. He need not have worried, for the dirty hands, noisy lapping of the tongue and snake-like licking of the dirty fingers would all have put Ma Palagada off from accepting anyway.

When Okolie had gone halfway through the food, and was resting from the great speed of his consumption, he started to make conversation.

"We eat a lot in our family. We enjoy lots of food, because I come from the house of a big man."

"Do you?" encouraged Ma Palagada.

"Yes, whenever Father caught any bush meat, we always finished it the same night. It used to be delicious." He waited for Ma Palagada to dispute this, but she did not.

She was used to Ibuza people, the way they talked. Every beggar from Ibuza was either a great person or the son or daughter of a great Somebody. The claims they made to those outside the town

66

made Ibuza sound like a unique place full of rich chiefs. Nobody there was poor, according to Ibuza's sons and grandsons. Ma Palagada had seen many of them in Asaba and in Onitsha itself. The fact that her own parents originally came from Ibuza made this man's bragging all the more ridiculous. His father might be the diokpa or the richest and oldest chief in Ibuza (if there was such a person) but, she observed, the way he gobbled his food gave no indication of someone from a well-fed home; on the contrary, it showed that there had never been soup to spare in his family, otherwise he would have known better than to lick his soup up like an animal, not a human being.

When he had almost finished, she felt it was time to start negotiations. She gave a polite cough to attract Okolie's attention as he was busy attacking the piece of chunky meat with his strong white teeth. In doing this he had hunched his broad shoulders so that they looked even wider and stronger; they seemed to taper into his arms and finish up with hands which though by no means small seemed diminutive in comparison with the muscular upper arms and shoulders. Okolie got the message and almost immediately started to splutter and rush his words in between mouthfuls.

From the intelligible parts of what he was saying, Ma Palagada was able to gather that he would take nothing less than twenty English pound notes for his "strong, well fed and healthy" sister.

"Because," he continued, "when she grows up, after serving you for all those years, you can give her away to any man you fancy and get your twenty pounds back. That is the minimum price we pay for brides in Ibuza, you know."

His listener knew all this and nodded tolerantly; but what she had to tell him after a long pause was that she was not going to pay a penny over seven pounds for the girl.

Okolie's earlier geniality evaporated. The last piece of meat he was chewing seemed about to choke him. He stared at his "relative" with horror.

"You want some more palm wine to wash down the offending piece of meat, relative?" she enquired solicitously.

He shook his head. There was nothing wrong with the meat; but there was something wrong with what Ma Palagada was saying. He spread his black hands this way and that way, asking the god Olisa to be his witness that he would never sell his dear sister for a sum so small.

"Do we look all that poor to you? Do we look like beggars, for

67

you to think that I can make this long journey just to sell my only sister for such a small amount. Thank you for the food, but now I will have to go back to your stall and take back my dear little sister. She must be missing me."

"Drink some more wine, Okolie, or you will choke."

"Do you think you will be able to buy her against my better judgement, after making me drink a lot of palm wine? No, you are wrong. I am not selling my sister for seven pounds. I must go and get her. . . ."

"Stop shouting. We are not quarrelling, relative — we are relatives, or have you forgotten? You must remember that to me she would never really be a slave. Do you forget that my mother and your father were from the same Eke market? That they both played under the same trees and rolled on the same sands? Then calm down. You're shouting like a village youth who has never seen money before. I don't want argument."

With a great deal of fussing about, she began to unwind the money belt she had wound round her waist. Most market women carried their money hidden in this way, with the belt then tied on top of their under lappa, which acted as an inner skirt, so that it was impossible for it to be grabbed by any thief. Slowly and laboriously Ma Palagada counted out the seven pounds, laid them in a nice neat pile under Okolie's nose.

The latter's protestations became weaker as each pound note was carefully rolled from the belt and smoothed out on the mat on which the food had been laid. Okolie looked askance but he was plainly fascinated. He could not remember seeing so many English notes piled together. His eyes began to water and to flicker this way and that, seemingly about to pop out of his head. He pushed away the food bowls, washed his hands and dried them on the inner cloth that was serving as underwear on this trip to Onitsha. Ma Palagada stopped counting at seven, and made as if to get up. It was now Okolie's turn to do the pleading.

"Don't rush so, little mother. Please sit, and let us go through this very carefully. You see, I have a coming-of-age dance and I am the chief dancer of the Uloko group. I do not want to look shabbily dressed on the day. I need more scarves than most of the dancers, and the number of my beads and anklets must triple that of the others, because all eyes will be on me. This money is too small to prepare me."

"Is that why you are selling her to me — just for your silly

68

dance?" Ma Palagada was beginning to lose her temper.

Okolie realised that the time was approaching for him to act quickly. Then he whined placatingly: "Add something more, please . . . more. . . ."

Ma Palagada was on her feet. She flung down a ten-shilling note, which she had kept in her sleeve for the purpose, and watched the effect. Okolie was still whining and gesticulating pathetically, and asking her how she thought he was going to manage to buy yam seeds, with the little she was offering, after his coming-of-age dance?

Ma Palagada bent down in a mock attempt to take back all the money, but Okolie was faster. He made a dive for it and quickly hid the notes in his *otuogwu*. Then Ma Palagada added her master stroke, which even she found most amusing when she later recalled it. When Okolie grabbed the money, she made a big show of walking away; however, she wanted to make quite sure he would not follow her back to her stall with his complaints and hard-luck stories. She turned and walked back abruptly, so much so that Okolie was afraid she was coming back to retrieve the money and he cowered back, clutching the pound notes under his cloth to his heaving breast, his eyes bulging with genuine apprehension. But all Ma Palagada wanted to do was to humiliate this greedy man from Ibuza so that he would not come to her again begging for pennies. His fate, she had since realised, was in his own hands: if he would not use those muscular arms in farming, if all he wanted to spend his life doing was blowing a horn pipe, that was his choice. All she was concerned with was that she was buying Ojebeta and did not want any strings attached. She was buying her outright, once and for ever, and that talk about being relatives was just shop talk. Would Okolie have thought of her if she had not made good in business? She dipped her hands into the loose end of her money belt and took out exactly enough shillings and sixpences to make up a round sum of another ten shillings, and thrust the coins on the table in front of Okolie, so that half of them rolled about on the mud floor of the stall.

She had looked back just once, when she was about to turn one of the innumerable corners that would lead to her own stalls, and saw him scrambling under the low eating benches and the mat tables in search of the shillings and sixpences. She laughed to herself once more.

The amusement soon disappeared from her face when she reached the last corner before her stall and heard Ma Mee calling.

"Palagada, Palagada, come into my stall. I want a word with you. Come."

Ma Palagada was not unaware of the other women cloth sellers who popped their heads out of their stalls at the sound of her name. Ma Palagada, like her neighbour Ma Mee, was a huge market mammy; in fact they were probably as heavy as each other, though Ma Palagada was not as broad. What might not be at first noticed, for her bulk robbed her of the effect of height, was that Ma Palagada was a very tall woman. So tall was she that people thought she was all legs. They said that when she dropped those legs in walking they went *palagada, palagada*, like kolanut pods falling on dry leaves; and because of this onomatopoeic description of how she threw those long legs forward the explosive name "Palagada", which was not the name her parents had given her, stuck. So popular and so wealthy, so charitable was she in her Christian beliefs, that anybody connected with her took on the same name. Her domestic slaves were Palagada girls or Palagada men, her children by her two husbands were Palagadas, and even her last husband, who came from over the sea and spoke Ibo in a funny way, was known locally as Pa Palagada.

She had to bend her great height almost double as she went into Ma Mee's stalls. Anyone outside, without knowing exactly what the latter told her, could be sure that it made Ma Palagada really angry. One might guess that Ma Mee had given a piece of unsought for advice — the type some people give instead of coming straight out and saying they are jealous of what you have. Of course, Ma Mee would have told her that it was for her own good, that had it not been for her Ma Palagada's new slave girl would have run into the market screaming for her brother, with those ridiculous bells ringing and ringing, and the big girl shouting, "Please stop her, she is our new slave!" She would have asked whether Ma Palagada was not being rather careless, for did she not know that trading in slaves had been abolished and that the few people who were still bought were bought secretly? (Ma Mee used occasions like this to get her own back for the envious gossip that circulated about her strategic position in the market.) It was not, of course (she would have hastened to add), that she begrudged Ma Palagada anything, it was simply that she felt they had known each other for such a long time that it was her duty more than anyone else's in Onitsha Otu to tell Ma Palagada the truth.

Ma Palagada thanked her, bustled away in anger and immediately

70

thundered at her girls, who were too frightened even to explain to her what had happened. She already seemed to have the version of the story she wanted to believe. They huddled together, and it was Chiago who bore the whole blame.

"Why did you let that bush untamed thing shout about the market like that? Were you all sleeping to let her out of your sight? And who told you she is a slave?" She did not enlighten them that Ojebeta came from the same place as her own parents; a statement like that could be used against her in a place like Otu market. "As for you," she went on, to Ojebeta, "when we get home, I am sending you up to Pa Palagada. He would certainly like to meet you after a performance like this."

"Ah, ah!" the other girls gasped, for to them Pa Palagada meant big punishment.

"What were you shouting for like that, eh? Were you hungry? Didn't you know where your brother was, eh? So why were you shouting, eh?"

Ojebeta shook her head negatively to these questions, backing away from Ma Palagada as far as possible. Fear had driven from her head all thoughts of asking to be taken home again. For once she began to be afraid of being physically punished, for she guessed somehow that if she went anywhere near this irate woman she would be beaten. So she stood almost hidden behind one of the many pieces of material hung up for sale.

Now Ma Palagada thundered again at Chiago, "Take her away from my cloth — she will make it dirty. Take her to the blacksmiths' stalls and let them file off all that junk she has tied all over her. Make sure you hold her tightly so that those stupid bells don't ring and those cowries make that pagan music."

She threw some pennies down on the mud floor for Chiago to pick up, which the latter did hurriedly, pulling Ojebeta like a dog behind her as they ran to the smiths' stalls.

Ojebeta could cry no more. She saw the charms which had been tied on her by her loving parents, to guide her from the bad spirits of the other world, filed painfully away. The cowries, too, which hung on banana strings were cut off with a big curved knife. She now cried in her heart which was throbbing up and down as though it would burst, as the hard lesson made itself clear to her that from this moment on she was alone.

Her survival depended on herself.

"May I take them with me?" she begged the blacksmith when he

71

had finished sawing the metals that held her charms together. "Please. . . ."

"I don't need them, little girl. You'd better ask your guide."

Chiago smiled through wet eyes but told her, "I'll be in trouble if I let you have them. What do you want them for anyway? They are dirty. You don't need them anymore."

"But my mother and my father gave them to me. I don't want to lose them. Please can I keep them. Your mother, there in the stall, she won't see them. Please. . . ."

Chiago looked helplessly at the little girl who was doing her utmost to cling on to her individuality. She did not yet know that no slave retained any identity: whatever identity they had was forfeited the day money was paid for them. She did not wish to rob this child of the small shred of self-respect she still had.

"Have them, but you must hide them in your *npe* — you must hide them so well that no one will see them. If they do see them, I'll say that I didn't know when you took them."

The ghost of a smile crossed Ojebeta's tear-stained face and for a moment illuminated her swollen eyes. She might have lost her identity, but at least she could still hold on to the dream of it.

They started back to the stalls, and Ojebeta found that it felt strange to walk without the charms that from birth had been tied on both her arms and her back. It was going to be difficult for her to walk and swing her arms like everybody else. It was going to take her a long time to learn to be somebody else.

7 Okolie and his Secret

Okolie, with his big *otuogwu* spread about him, was still looking in every corner of the food shed, to see if by chance he had missed any more pennies that Ma Palagada had thrown down there. In the intensity of his search he forgot his dignity, forgot what it was he had done. All the human pride he had — pride that he was a man, pride that he was the best horn blower of his age-group, pride that he was Ibuza's greatest orator — all was submerged in his urge to find money, and more money. His attitude recalled those days when it was easy for the European to urge the chief of a powerful village to wage war on a weaker one in order to obtain slaves for the New World.

After looking and crawling about and scratching the beaten mud floor with his claw-like fingers, Okolie started muttering to himself, his mouth watering at the suggestion from his fertile imagination that there must surely be more money somewhere ready for him to happen upon. One of the girls who worked there had been bringing a tired customer to that section where our optimistic Okolie was busy searching, but she restrained the customer from entering the shed and pointed wordlessly to this grown man grovelling on his hands and knees. They heard him murmuring, saw the anxiety in his eyes, they sensed his deep concentration and they watched. Naturally, their standing there by the entrance of the shed attracted other girls, who were normally overworked at this time of day when the market was nearing its close; it was now that traders, buyers, ordinary market people liked to fill their bellies at the food stalls before starting their long homeward journeys to the various villages from which they had travelled. The girls, most of whom were house servants or slaves, welcomed a diversion of this sort, and a small crowd soon gathered. So engrossed was Okolie in his hunt for treasure that he was oblivious to it all.

The first girl, having watched Okolie longer than the others there, suddenly realised that he was not a mad man but simply a greedy one. Her suspicions were buttressed by the fact that she had heard some of the haggling that had gone on between Okolie and Ma Palagada, and by the fact that from time to time as he crawled Okolie would check in his cloth to make sure that the bulk of the money was still there. She burst out laughing. The bearded trader standing beside her also laughed loud and rich. Most of the people standing there watching began to laugh as well.

"Have you lost something, big man from Agbor?" one girl's voice asked laughingly. Because Okolie was wearing his best white *otuogwu*, the type of garment which all Ibos west of the Niger wore for ceremonial occasions, she had simply mentioned Agbor as the biggest town further into the interior that she could think of. It just would not have occurred to her that a person from so near a place as Asaba or Ibuza could behave in such a low fashion; no, he must surely be from the very interior of the Western Ibo region, near Benin.

Okolie clambered up and looked wildly about him. So lost was he in his money dream that it took him a few seconds to realise that he was there in the biggest market in that part of the country, and that he, the son of a well known person in his town, was being watched scratching about the market floor looking for coins. He knew the way he must look. Suppose somebody who knew him, his people, his family, should be among this crowd? He must make a dash for it, and leave as fast as his legs could carry him.

Voices rang out ridiculing him the more.

"Are you from Ogbaru?"

"Oh, no, he is from the bush somewhere."

"Are you from Okpanam?" they laughed.

He did not wish to reply. He knew the power of the crowd. They could attack him, pull his cloth from him and take the money away. He edged his way out, feeling lucky that the crowd was still in a teasing mood though fast working itself up into a violent one. Before anyone could suggest that he might be a market thief, Okolie had mingled with the throng. Instinct told him to remove his ceremonial cloth and wrap it securely round the money, and he continued through the market in his under wrapper, looking like a canoe man.

At the waterside he was not surprised to see that all the steamers run by marine engines had already gone. He had dreamed of making

74

his return journey to Ibuza in one of these sophisticated steamers that raced through the water without the help of paddles. But he was too late; in fact the last one, called *Ericho*, was just about to leave but was too full to think of taking on an extra passenger. With much misgiving and disappointment, he decided to take one of the canoes, known as *ugbo-amala*, paddled by men from Olunmili.

The sun had gone down completely, and the market was busy emptying itself. A crowd of late Western Ibos had gathered on the bank ready to cross the river. Groups of Eastern Ibos were making their way up the hills into their home villages. As far as trading went, there was a new wind blowing, and keen Ibo traders let themselves be blown along by it. The exporting of slaves, which had boosted the fortunes of many in places such as Opobo and Bonny, had ended, and now the emphasis had switched to palm oil and palm kernels. It was not a trade that was limited to the Ibos along the coast. Even a poor boy miles away in the interior could gain from it. He could go into the bush to collect the kernels, come home to his hut and crush the shells between two stones; then he could tie the whole palm fruits that had been so shelled and take them to the Otu market. The middle men, who did not allow the Europeans to come inland, would buy these bags of palm fruits for a few shillings each, load them on to steamers or canoes which would carry them to big ports like Port Harcourt. From there the kernels went to Europe to be made into things like soap.

It was these small boy traders and poor women who waited till the very end of the market, hoping to get just a penny or so more for their bags of kernels. They had put so much time and energy into collecting and shelling the kernels that they preferred to go home by the cheaper canoes, which cost only a penny per passenger, than by the engined steamers which charged sixpence a crossing. In Okolie's case it had been his haggling over the price for his sister that had delayed him.

He saw a little girl, not much older than Ojebeta, struggling into the canoe which he himself was boarding. Her mother called to her to watch her step and not tumble into the water. Friendly hands stretched out towards her to help her jump in.

He felt he had to ask the mother, "Why did you bring her to Otu?"

She had smiled with triumph and explained, "She sold all her kernels, and she wanted to choose her first European lappa for herself. So I brought her to make her selection."

75

The little girl nodded happily at Okolie, proudly showing him a folded piece of material.

So mixed were his feelings that at first laughter threatened, then tears. He had a hard time controlling himself from confessing to this seemingly poor mother and child: "Look, it took my mother over fifteen years to placate the gods, before she had the little girl that she wanted so much to be her companion, her daughter, her friend and her very own. And do you know what I have done? I have sold her to a rich woman who is distantly related to us, for eight pounds — and, see, I have the money here with me. Do you think I have done wrong?"

His thoughts were so full of this that he was gazing long and hard at the little girl and, even though it was getting fairly dark, the mother made out his expression and wondered why this strange man was staring at her like that.

"Come, daughter," she told her child, "why don't you sit on this side and let me sit there, near our new friend."

Okolie did not wish to harm the little girl, and he knew that at that moment his thoughts of his sister showed on his face. Who, he wondered, would offer her a friendly hand as someone had to this little girl? Who would encourage her to save her first earnings to buy herself a new European cloth? Who would call her by her pet names and tell her she was prettier than the queen of Idu, who would show her the farm that used to belong to their father, and tell her what he used to say and what he used to do? Okolie shed a silent tear of remorse, grateful that the darkness would hide it. But he soon felt comforted when his hands involuntarily touched the rustling English notes in his *otuogwu*. He told himself that Ojebeta would be well looked after. "If she had stayed with me, she would probably die of felenza, and if not felenza then something much more terrible. For who would look after her other than our aunt with the husband with watery eyes?"

Of course he meant Uteh, who at that moment was sitting with her husband Eze inside Okolie's bachelor hut waiting for his return. Another relative, Ukabegwu, whose wife had run away from him because he had an offensive sore foot, later joined them there, bringing with him some pieces of kolanut. They sat there on the mud seat in Okolie's hut and talked of many things, of the terrible epidemic, and of the fact that that year's yam festival was going to be a sham.

"For where are the men to do the strong dances with the bamboo shields? All our men are gone," lamented Uteh.

"Don't despair, cousin," said Ukabegwu. "Men come and men go, just like the waves of the sea. I remember the Ifejioku festival of only last year — the noise, the food, the children, the men . . . so many people. Most of them are gone now. Even the children, but there are some of us left to carry on the work of producing more and more children. And that is why I am now begging our mother of the Oboshi river, the great guardian of the Eke market and your *chi* to give you a male child, so that the name of your husband can be remembered."

They all clapped the palms of their hands together, saying, *"Ise. Ise.* Let it be so."

Eze felt that he had to pray for his in-law too, and even prayer to the gods he did in a funny way, like everything else.

"Yes, we pray for you too," he said. "For God to take away this horrible sore of yours that has gone green and smells so badly that your wife will not come home. After all, you are not a greater sinner than any of us. . . . Or did you steal God's wife? What have you done to deserve this lot?"

Ukabegwu and Uteh did not know how to say *"Ise"* to this prayer. Uteh kept quiet, though after a while Ukabegwu said, "I see what you mean. But I simply have to accept my lot, just as you have accepted yours. My wife ran away to her people with two children, a boy and a girl; the girl died of felenza last week, but — who knows? — the boy may be spared. Let us pray to God to spare him for us, so that he may live and be a great man, a great hunter and a great Obi."

Before husband and wife could decide whether to say *"Ise"* to this, Ukabegwu had already said it himself and had taken a deep bite into the piece of kolanut in his hand to show that he had sealed the prayer with the gods. For among those people there was a saying that if you tell your neighbour that your arm is hurting you, he will turn round and say to you that it is not only your arm that should be hurting you, but your leg and your head also. As far as Ukabegwu was concerned, these people were trying to tell him that he was a hungry man, and instead of accepting that he extended his stomach to them, telling them that in fact he was too full.

The truth of the matter, however, was that Uteh and her husband accepted him as he rated himself, proving another saying that if you laugh, the world laughs with you.

Eze thought for a while — it was obvious that he was thinking from the way he rubbed his bad eye. Then he patted his in-law on the shoulder and said: "You are a great man, Maduka the son of Ukabegwu."

"Thank you. We do not breed idiots in our family."

The silence that followed this was very long, even among sworn enemies.

Eze was not unaware of the name his wife's family called him behind his back. He was beginning to blame himself for coming to his in-law's place this dark evening just because his wife wanted to take Ojebeta with her. After all, a girl needed men to guide her: her father, or any man who could represent a father to her, or when she grew up a husband. So was not her brother the rightful person to decide the fate of little Ojebeta? Yet he, Eze, was sitting here now listening to himself being insulted by this man with the smelly foot, just for poking his eyes into something that was not his business.

Aloud he said, "We have to go soon if your kinsman Okolie is not coming back."

"Please, wait a little longer to be my company. Since the ravages of felenza this place has become very quiet when Okolie is away like this. When he is in, his friends come here to blow their horn pipes, and Ojebeta chatters away around him. . . ."

He stopped abruptly, for whose head should they see poking inside the dimly lit hut but that of Okolie himself.

"You are going to live long," Ukabegwu said, "for we were just talking about you."

"Why shouldn't I live long? I have done nobody any harm," Okolie was quick to point out.

His tone was too sharp for the light conversation. After all, it had simply been a reference to one of their widely held superstitions, that if you were talking about someone and he suddenly appeared, it showed that he was going to have a long life. Or if you talked of someone far away, that person would sneeze, wherever he was. And similarly, sudden and early death could often be proof that you were not a very good person; if, for example, a man was struck by lightning, the belief was that he had been having an affair with someone else's wife.

Uteh remarked that Okolie must be very tired; but Eze, not taking his wife's hint, came straight to the point.

"I promised Ojebeta this morning that her big mother would be bringing her pounded yam when she returned from Asaba. Now we are here with the food, but where is the little girl?"

Uteh knew that she would have to accept any explanation Okolie gave them about Ojebeta. She did not want to go into details about it, not in front of her husband, for she must try to protect the name of her family even from the man she was married to. In Ibuza if one member of a family stole, the whole family were regarded as thieves. If there were witches in one branch of a village, the whole village would be known as a bad place and full of witches. So if you did not want people to call you names, you did not wash the family's dirty cloth outside your hut, for if you did that the dirt might smear your own clean cloth, whether or not you even knew who the particular culprit was.

Okolie reacted abruptly, his voice sharp, his body tense like that of a watchful cat: "I thought I told you this morning that I was taking her to Adah Palagada? I thought I explained that to you." He sat down wearily on the mud seat facing his unwanted visitors. "I want my little sister to see the world, to learn how to trade, to be a successful trader like our kinswoman Adah Palagada."

Although Ma Palagada had married foreigners, who might not speak a word of Ibo, there was no denying that she was rich and a success, so they still considered her an *adah*, a daughter of the family.

Uteh felt limp. There would be a more opportune moment to look into the matter. She would go to Asaba or wherever the only daughter of Okwuekwu Oda was. She was not against her staying on to be brought up as a trader, but Uteh would like to know on what terms.

After that day Okolie said no more about his sister, and indeed none of his kinsmen dared ask. It seemed that Uteh's earlier lament was true, that the felenza had carried away the men who were men; what they were left with were the ghosts of men. Besides, other important things began to occupy their minds. Ojebeta's name after a while was almost forgotten, so much so that some people muddled the facts and said she had died with her parents and been secretly buried. So short was the memory of people.

Okolie mourned the loss of his sister for days. His was not the kind of mourning that he could share with anyone. Had Ojebeta simply died, relatives and friends would have consoled and sympathised

79

with him. But this kind of loss burned his conscience. For days he could not eat properly. Once, he counted the money, patting each note and rubbing each piece of silver with his fingers, and feeling guilty. He knew that he was behaving wrongly not only in terms of himself and his little sister; more seriously, he was violating the custom. He had no right to claim any money that his sister might fetch. Now that their father was dead, her bride price when she grew up belonged by right to his older brother Owezim. Okolie's share would have been a pound or so; but now, not only had he sold his sister for less than half the price she would later have had paid for her in marriage, he was also keeping all that money for himself. That was the type of sin, he realised, that you knew you were committing with your eyes open, and the type that must die with you.

Involuntarily he hoped his sister would never come back to tell the story and that his adventurous brother, who had seen the signs of things to come and had gone to one of the newly developing towns, would be so successful in his search for riches that an amount like eight pounds would be of little consequence to him. After a few days he even began to believe that what he hoped for had happened, that his sister had died — and even if she was an only daughter, she was still only a daughter — and that his elder brother had made enough money in whatever part of the world he was doing his whiteman's job. So was Okolie's conscience steeled by time.

The day of the big coming-out dance of his age-group was fast approaching, and there were signs that the felenza had done its worst, though people were still dying, and some still emigrated to what was known as "olu oyibo", white men's work. As a result of the loss sustained by his age-group Okolie became not only the chief horn blower but also the leader of the dancers. Awun-nta — "Mosquito" — previously the natural dance leader because of his long, skinny legs and his lightness, had also emigrated to the hills of the Hausas where it was said that not only were there jobs but the felenza disease did not kill as many people as it did in Ibuza. So Okolie benefited socially and in reputation from the misfortune of others in his age-group. It was essential for him to maintain the prestige of this position, and to do so was costly — which was where Ojebeta's money helped. He bought the most colourful scarves to tie round his waist for the dance, scarves that were so expensive and so modern that women gaped in awe wondering how he could afford it all.

It was with the coming of the rain that felenza seemed to have been washed away, no one quite knew how. All they knew was that the sudden deaths that had been occurring, day in, day out, slowed down and people were gradually returning to their farms. One night there had been the kind of thunderstorm Ibuza had never before experienced. It had gone on for hours; trees were uprooted, branches torn off, and hailstones fell at random. People shivered and wondered. Okolie was in his bachelor hut practising his horn pipe with some of his dancing group, and the roof of the hut was shaking as if the wind wanted to tear it away.

Ukabegwu came in and said pessimistically, "Maybe those of us left are to be swept away by the storm."

"Stop talking in childish riddles, old man," one of Okolie's friends remarked. "We must have our coming-of-age celebration like every other age-group since Ibuza was founded. Why should the gods deny us our turn?"

Okolie replied by blowing his horn pipe as loudly as he could, and the shrill notes seemed to wake the gods of rain into action again. Rain poured from the sky, as if the whole of the heavens had opened up in alarm and let out all the waters they were holding. It poured the whole night, so heavily that Okolie's friends stayed in his hut rather than try to reach their own.

But in the morning there were no more tears, for there were no more deaths. Not only that, but the maize plants and the few yams that had been planted were given an unexpected boost by this late watering, for before there had been little rain, and many farmers had given up hope. The few elders who had survived knew, however, that it would be two or three months after the yam festival that food would start becoming scarce and expensive, and more people would die from famine. Had not all their able farmers been plucked away in their prime by untimely deaths? And was it not true that those who remained alive seemed to be the lazy ones? Even those few who had struggled hard with their farms had not had rains at the right time, though this late rain revived some hope.

More yams survived for that harvest season than people expected, and it was felt that they would celebrate the yam festival as best they could, though the commemorative coming-out dance and the other dances that year promised to be nothing compared to what they used to be, when the main road to Ibuza from Umuodafe to Ogbeowele would be packed with people of different ages.

On the night before Okolie's Uloko dance, his aunt Uteh left her husband's house and came to stay with Okolie for she reasoned, "I am his living mother." She did not mind that there were other young men there practising and preparing themselves with him. She had brought enough yams to last him through the whole period of his coming-out dance, and one of the young men, seeing Uteh sitting there and suspecting that she intended to spend the whole night, asked Okolie in confidence,

"But look, our horn blower — no one is supposed to see this dance before the day. Your little mother is here watching it all."

"She is not my little mother, she is the only mother I have left. Can you order your own mother out of your hut? What are you talking about?"

His friend grumbled but knew better than to stir up trouble, for Okolie was the only horn player they had.

On the day, Okolie came out in style. Round his head he wrapped a red silk scarf with card patterns on it and round his waist, instead of ordinary raffia, were many more scarves of every colour, yellow, black, green, grey. All this topped the kind of george material that had never before been seen in Ibuza, with a brown background with yellow workings on it, some resembling birds, some leaves, some snakes. Even for his ankle beads he did not use the shells of nuts as others did but had small copper bells that rang out when he danced.

Uteh too was not to be left behind, and was wearing the best *otuogwu* in her possession and had a special feather fan with pieces of mirror wedged in it. She, together with most of the other relatives from Umuisagba, followed Okolie, singing his praise names.

Before Okolie set out, he went to perform the first steps of his new dances to his parents. After a few such steps at his father's burial place, he stood like a mighty bird in curtsy and said, "Father, guide me from the eyes of witches and other evil people. I dance for you to approve of me before any other person because you gave me life." Since his mother had died while still in mourning, custom had demanded that her body be thrown into the "bad bush", and though Okolie could not go there, with tears in his eyes he repeated the same words to his mother.

Ukabegwu, the only living elder among Okolie's kinsmen, saw what was happening and shouted: "The dead will guide us. Leave them alone. Is not today the best day of your life? Come, do not be moody. Celebrate it with life." The old man brought a big bottle of the home-made gin known as Ogogoro, poured a lot on the bodies of all the relatives and made Okolie drink a great deal of it. All his kinsmen also had at least four mouthfuls each, and the transformation was noticeable.

Okolie blew his horn pipe until his cheeks looked as if they would burst. Uteh sang his praise names, not only for the living to hear but also for the dead, and even the gods. The few children danced as if they had winged feet. Old women remembered their own coming-out days, and shook and wriggled their dry bodies with excitement, showing their sparse tobacco-blackened teeth. As for the young girls of Umuisagba, no young man did they spoil as much as they did Okolie on this big day. They took pieces of colourful material, left over from some tailor's shop and cut into "handiker-shishi", and waved these in the air whenever Okolie blew his pipe; and when he started to dance, jumping and looping to the rhythm of the music, they would run in and out of the ring where he was and wipe the sweat from his face, his body and his arms.

Uteh never tired of fanning him with her feather fan and saying, "Look at him, a young man as strong as the strongest tiger, as fast as the arrows of the gods. Whose son is he? He is the son of Okwuekwu Oda, the man with the golden voice, the man who carried the European on his shoulder, the man who walked to Idu and talked with the king of Idu. He is not rich, he is not poor, but he is satisfied. Look at him — have you ever seen a horn blower like this one? . . ." On and on she went, until they joined the other members of the group from other parts of Ibuza.

By the time they had danced round Ibuza, many relatives from Okolie's mother's side had joined in singing his praise names. One old woman from Ezukwu who had looked after his mother Umeadi as a child came out and said:

"Who was born in the centre of the biggest market in Ibuza?"

"He!" the crowd replied. Fingers pointed at Okolie, and the voice of the crowd was as heavy as the blast of a gun, as frightening as claps of thunder.

She went on: "Who makes the earth shake when he walks?"

"He!"

"Who has a body like those of the polished images made by wood carvers?"

"He!"

"Who is going to be the greatest farmer of his time?"

"He, he, he is now going to be the greatest farmer — 'Ugbo Ukwu', the young man with the biggest farm."

People applauded and Okolie danced and blew his gratitude to the women; singers sang her praise names and she, despite a painful knee, managed to make some mock steps, to the happiness of everyone around.

Okolie told himself that it had all been worth it. For days and years afterwards people would still be talking about it and saying, "Do you know that when Okolie Ugbo Ukwu came out, he was the best dressed man, the best dressed dancer and the best horn blower of his time?"

So before the end of a season Okolie had acquired a title, but one he knew he could not live up to. What was more, he had so impressed the girls, with his dancing and his well-fed body and his expensive outfit, that he was forced to accept the gift of a wife.

Although he protested to the girl's parents that he could not pay the bride price, the elders of her people laughed and said, "Only a foolish man would admit that he is rich. A rich man does not tell people he is rich but his behaviour says as much." Okolie did not know whether to run away or bury himself alive.

"Are you impotent?" his only living relative questioned him. "Why do you protest so much? The girl ran to you after watching you dance, her people did not mind, she is beautiful with lovely skin, and you still say no. Why? Have you ever come across someone who is too much of a coward to eat a piece of cooked fish that is put into his mouth? Eat it, and eat it fast, or else those who called you 'Ugbo Ukwu' yesterday will give you another name, Okolie Ujo Ugbo — Okolie the farm truant."

So Okolie was forced to do what was expected of him on that score. He even bought yam roots with what was left over of the money he had received for selling his sister.

But is there not a saying that there are those who are born to lead and those who are born to be led? Indeed, Okolie had the height of a near giant, his skin shone like painted ebony, his waist was as small as that of a snake and his shoulders were like those of two men put together. He also had the energy of three men. But he was not born to use all this.

Okolie was one of those born to make excuses.

He spent all the money, and his yam did not grow, for he could not get up regularly as the other farmers did to tend the young plants. Within a year he was in debt with his in-laws; he could not afford to pay the bride price of his wife; his wife did not conceive and people wondered why. She was becoming dry and thin and people knew that this was due to hunger. Okolie did not know what to do but to put the blame on felenza, on his elder brother for going away and leaving him, and on his wife for running to him at all.

Then came the inevitable famine. What saved many people when yam failed was that some Europeans who had been to Brazil introduced the cassava root to that part of the world. At first the Ibuza people were suspicious of it, and they gave it, as they did all new food, to the old people to eat first. When they enjoyed it and thrived, everyone else took to it. But even cassava needed a man to plant it. Kwufo, Okolie's wife, did her best; but Okolie could not cope.

In the end, he too sneaked away one night in search of a "white man's job".

8 The Palagadas

Time is always said to be a great healer of wounds, however deep they may be when fresh, and Ojebeta's case was no exception. She had one great advantage over many others who suffer loss: she had youth.

For days she had cried silently, since the joy of letting others know your sorrows was denied slaves like her. Nobody actually told her she must not talk about her past; circumstances simply made it impossible to do so or even to think about it. What time was there to think about yourself when as soon as the first cock crowed, around five in the morning, a loud bell was sounded by the big male slave called Jienuaka. If by this time you were still asleep, a biting whip slashed round your body, and you jumped up, and ran like a wild animal let out of a cage, wriggling with pain. You could be the early age of four or a mature slave of thirty, the same treatment applied. At the time Ojebeta went there she was seven.

She had soon learned to be up even before Jienuaka rang his monstrous bell. They would all take their cans and rush to the stream to fetch the household water. The mornings were usually dewy and wet, so you tied your house lappa and wore an old blouse. At the stream you bathed and then walked back home, sometimes half asleep all the time, though the stream was not far away, only three miles from where they lived at the Palagada mansion.

Ojebeta's first sight of the Palagada mansion was one of the wonders of the day she first came to Onitsha that she thought would stick forever in her memory. On that first day, after her impulsive attempt to run away had been foiled, Ojebeta had stood, like a mechanical doll that had no life in it except when wound up, until they told her it was time to go home. Ma Palagada had asked, in the tones of someone used to having her orders obeyed in seconds, and without taking her eyes off Ojebeta:

"Have you any left-over abada today, one or two waist wraps?"

The question had not been particularly addressed to any one of the girls, but a dark skinny girl with heavy lips, who looked a little ill and unhappy and had been silent all afternoon, came temporarily to life as she answered her mistress: "We have a wrap of some Opobo cloth left. It has been left over for three markets now."

"Thank you, Nwayinuzo." Her name which meant "a girl found by the wayside" sounded appropriate as Ma Palagada said it. "Bring it and tie it round the girl. Her name is Ojebeta, did you get that? Ojebeta. . . ."

The four girls looked at Ojebeta as if they had just seen her. All Ojebeta saw was a group of girls who behaved so quietly, as if frightened for their lives. She did not know then that she too, Ojebeta the only daughter of Umeadi, who had been encouraged to trust everybody, to say what she felt like saying, to shout when she felt like doing so, would start behaving like these girls who so reminded her of the wooden dolls in front of her *chi* shrine at home in Ibuza. Nwayinuzo meanwhile had brought out some attractive material with red, yellow and brown lines running through it. She had told Ojebeta to throw away her *npe* and wrap this material round her body, and had knotted the two ends of the wrapper at the back of Ojebeta's neck. She had felt quite pleased with herself; but she still clutched her charms under her arm, tucked inside her *npe* which her mother had woven herself, and which now looked crude and unrefined next to this soft, smooth material they had wound round her.

Then they had proceeded home, balancing the piles of unsold cloth on their heads. The procession went in ascending order of age and rank, with the younger immature slaves at the front so that they could not try to run away, and with their owner Ma Palagada bringing up the rear. Ojebeta was given four bundles of cloth to carry, one on top of the other.

They soon left the waterside and the dense heat of the noisy market, and walked along a road that ran parallel to the river, where there were swaying palms that wafted refreshing clean breezes from the river and emptied it all on them. Then they branched into a big road, the biggest Ojebeta had ever seen: it seemed as wide as the Eke market which until that day she had thought the biggest open space in the world. Again along this road — which she later learned to call the Old Market Road — were trees planted at regular intervals one from the other. It was all so wide and so airy

87

and so tidy that she wondered whether it could all possibly have been done by living people. Thinking again of her dead parents Ojebeta almost cried again. As for her brother Okolie, she tried to forget him. That he could leave her among these people, some of whom called her a slave while others called her a relative — he her only brother, whom she had trusted so completely — if he could do that and not so much as tell her what it was all about, it was better that she forgot him.

They began to pass some peculiar, really large houses. Her father had once taken her to see the Ibuza court, the school and the Catholic church, and those had been big houses with *akayan* palm leaves on their roofs, so big that they had several openings on each side to allow in air, as her father had explained. But the houses she was then seeing were even bigger than the Ibuza church, court and school all put together. She would have liked to linger and look at the houses; many of them had small bushes in front of them, and Ojebeta had never seen tamed vegetation before. She asked the girl walking close to her, who looked almost the same age as herself, what the houses were for.

The little girl had smiled, then, looking back to make sure Ma Palagada was not within earshot, said in a loud whisper, "People live there, rich people like us. Wait till you see our house. It's round that corner."

"Big mouth, big appetite and empty brain, Amanna," accused Nwayinuzo from the back, and then felt it her duty to report what Amanna was telling Ojebeta. But Ma Palagada simply laughed.

Before she finished laughing, they had turned a sharp corner and a road covered with red stones came into view. At the end of the road was the most beautiful house that Ojebeta had ever seen.

She held her breath, then exclaimed: "Mother and Father, come and see!" It was as she imagined the houses belonging to the sea goddesses she had heard of in so many fables.

The house was painted white. It had a whole row of tamed bushes in front of it, just like the ones they had seen along the main road. Everywhere there were large openings which she later learned to call windows. At the centre of the front of the house was a large door, high and wide enough to take a giant compared to the small doorways she had been impressed by in Ibuza. At the side there was another big door with two giant gates.

"This is our house," Amanna pointed out with pride and enthusiasm; so great was her adaptation and acceptance that she obvious-

88

ly really did look on it as her home. In fact she could not even remember what part of Calabar she had originally come from; it was Ma Palagada who had given her the Ibo name Amanna, meaning someone who did not know her own father. She had been born a twin among people who rejected twins, and though her mother had managed to nurse her secretly for a while, the time had come when it was impossible to keep her any longer, and the child was sold. Amanna did not know a word of her native Efik but chattered like a monkey in Ibo. Ojebeta later realised that Ma Palagada, although she bought slaves whom she expected to work hard to help her with her trade and with the running of her vast household, was not as strict a mistress as others, and even seemed to try as much as possible to treat her girl slaves as her own daughters — "as much as possible", because no well brought up lady in her situation would, for example, dream of allowing her bought girls to sleep in the same building as the daughters of "human beings": there were special parts of the compound allocated to them.

At the front of the mansion Ojebeta had seen a man dressed in khaki shorts and white jacket who rushed to open the big door for Ma Palagada to pass through. Ojebeta stood there for a while, watching wide-mouthed as the other girls made their way into the compound by a side gate.

"Come, here, little girl from Ibuza, or are you sleeping?" Amanna called.

Ojebeta woke up and ran after them, almost dropping her charms which she had concealed in her new lappa. Ojebeta looked alarmed, but if Ma Palagada had noticed anything she said nothing, perhaps thinking that it would help Ojebeta to settle down, knowing that her native *ogbanje* charms were still with her. Those charms did indeed give Ojebeta great comfort. Each one of them she came to identify with a particular member of her family as she had known it as a child. The biggest bell was her father, the next in line her mother. Two cowries were her brothers. Her mother's friends and her aunt Uteh were all there. When things became difficult she would call upon them one by one to help her out. In the days when she was new the others girls laughed and made fun of her over this, but she ignored them. And later they came to regard Ojebeta's charms with something bordering on awe. She was soon accepted, this strange little dark-skinned newcomer, charms and all.

But on that first day, she had concealed the charms quickly again, and joined the others going through the big gate by the side

89

of the house. The gate was wooden and painted a red wine colour, as were the frames of the windows. The top part of the main door was of glass and the bottom wooden part was painted, again in the same colour. Inside the yard was another small building which Ojebeta gathered belonged to them, the slaves, the house servants, the steward boys. The girls all shared one large room.

"This is my corner," Amanna had bubbled. "You will be sleeping on the same mat with me. But you'll have to throw your shells and bells away, otherwise they'll rattle and make so much noise that we won't get enough sleep."

"Yes," Nwayinuzo had put in, "you can't keep those funny things here. They stink."

"You still want to hang on to them?" Chiago asked in a cool voice, hating to deprive a little girl of the sole reminder that at one time she had had people of her own.

Ojebeta nodded vigorously. "I can keep them under my head. I'll look after them," she begged, so intensely that the others could not mistake how important they were to her. "My father bought them for me. He went to Idu to see the king, and he brought them for me. Please let me keep them."

"All right," Chiago compromised once more, "keep them. But no more attempts at running away. It's not so bad here. There's plenty of food, clean clothes and—"

"You won't have to wear pagan charms," teased Amanna. Ojebeta had felt unable to resist fighting this cheeky new friend she had acquired. She had made a move, but Chiago told her not to be silly. Then Amanna remarked that Ma Palagada had not reported Ojebeta to her husband, as she had promised.

"Yes, I think Ma has forgotten," agreed Chiago, "but don't let me catch you going up to the big house to remind her of it, otherwise I'll tell her that you still wet your mat."

Amanna thought about this for a second, then as she hurried to change into an old house lappa she commented, "It's not fair, though, because if it was me she would remember to send me up to the master, to be caned and punished for running away."

"Maybe you are sent up so often because you gossip so much, telling tales about what you saw, and what you didn't see, and what you will never see until you die. So shut up, and let's go and help in the kitchen," said Ijeoma as she began to walk out of the room. It was easy to see that she loved food, for she was a round girl with two deep dimples in her cheeks that showed clearly when

90

she laughed, which was quite frequently.

By night, their quarrels of the day had been forgotten and Ojebeta shared a mat with Amanna. She was too tired to brood long over her misfortune; she clung to her charms in the dark, knowing no one was watching.

The girl called Ijeoma — her name which meant "good journey" had been given to her by her captors who sold her: it was said she came from Arochukwu when her village was raided by robbers — shared a mat with Nwayinuzo but even Ojebeta could see that the latter was friendlier with Chiago, who had to sleep apart because she was older and their leader. She soon found out why Ijeoma was not very popular. She was very noisy, and always happy, and the Palagadas liked her for her outspokenness and her ability to work (which was not surprising, considering the amount she ate). But sleeping in the same room as her was hair-raising. How she snored! Nwayinuzo, since she had had to sleep with her, wore a special scarf at night which she tied over her ears to prevent her having to listen to Ijeoma's ceaseless snores. This did not bother Ijeoma, who said she did not know what she did when she went to sleep.

"Can you control your behaviour when you are asleep?" she asked in self-defence. "Sleep is like a little death, you know, in which you are lost to the land of the living, so how then can you help what you do?" she wanted to know. The others did not have an answer, so they let her be and simply put up with it; most of them were usually too tired to mind much anyway, or to spend the little time they had for sleep in unnecessary argument that led nowhere.

Amanna's bed-wetting was more disturbing. She had been caned several times for it, starved of food, of water, but all to no avail. It had become a habit. The responsibility for waking her up to go to the gutter in the back yard was Chiago's. But they had stopped reporting Amanna and just used the threat of it to make her behave. After all no one came to visit them, unless the Palagadas wanted to show special visitors their slaves' sleeping quarters, and they were told in time to tidy the room and let fresh air in to neutralise the wetness. To cap it all, right from the first day of her stay Ojebeta started wetting the mat too, she and Amanna became comrades in mat-wetting.

So for the next two or three years Amanna and Ojebeta nightly enjoyed the shared comfort of their mutual shame.

*   *   *

"I don't like the idea of going into his room at all when he comes to live here," Chiago was confiding to Nwayinuzo late one night. "They used to make me do that every morning. I had to go in there, empty his chamber-pot, wake him up and wish him good morning."

"Well, there's nothing wrong in that. You do that for Ma anyway, so what's so bad in doing the same for her son? I don't rem—"

"Oh, you were too young then. You don't understand. He fiddles with me. He used to make me do things. . . . O my *chi*, help me in this household."

Here Chiago broke down crying quietly in her sleeping clothes. She was trying hard to keep her anguish under control and Nwayinuzo was doing her best to comfort her broken-hearted friend.

"Sh . . . shh. . . . You mustn't cry so. You'll wake the others. . . ."

They both stopped talking for a while. Chiago reduced her cries to heart-rending sobs, and they both listened to the breathing of the three other sleeping girls. Ijeoma was snoring away as usual, having filled herself with another heavy cassava meal before going to bed; they watched her lying there on the mat she shared with Nwayinuzo, her feet spread wide apart, her plump head on her big breasts, her mouth hanging open. That girl was getting fatter every day, so fat, particularly round the belly, that one would have thought she had had babies; some of the traders who worked with Ma Palagada at Otu had given her the nickname "Mama Ijeoma". As for Amanna and her friend Ojebeta, at least they no longer disturbed the nights with their mat-wetting ritual, though even before those two outgrew the habit the older girls had anyway given up waking them to go outside.

Chiago, now seventeen, was normally a quiet girl, not used to telling people her thoughts, but tonight she was troubled by what she had learned in the big house earlier in the evening. Ma Palagada had obviously been feeling happy, and a little drunk. Pa Palagada had been very drunk, and drunkenness emphasised his overhanging stomach, his red eyes and his loud laughter. Chiago had heard their loud conversation, since only she and the male slave Jienuaka were allowed to serve in the big house during the evening meal.

"They say he has grown into a very tall young man," Ma Palagada was saying with pride.

"We are big people in my family — who else do you want Clifford to look like?" Pa Palagada thundered in amusement. This statement was greeted with a loud burst of laughter that sounded like the snorting noise made by an angry bull.

They had gone on talking about their children and they both agreed that they were indeed blessed by the good Lord to have such a handsome son and beautiful daughters. They admitted that their son could not make head nor tail of the new white man's learning, but what did he need such learning for? Such learning was for slaves, not the sons and daughters of real rich human beings like themselves.

"Ah, that reminds me," Ma Palagada put in as an afterthought. "The new U.A.C. chief and his wife are church people. I must make all our servants enrol in their Sunday school. They teach them to read the Ibo Bible and to sing hymns. I want them to see how our girls are treated."

"You can send the slave girls if you like, but I would not advise you to do the same with your flesh and blood daughters."

"No, of course not," his wife had readily agreed heartily.

Chiago had stayed in the household long enough to know that the daughters in question were Ma Palagada's children by a white "Potokis". They looked strange with their pale colour. Because they could not settle down properly with Pa Palagada they had been sent away somewhere to be trained in different kinds of learnings. Ma Palagada pretended to let her present husband make the rules. Her only son was by him, and the boy was as black as any of them; but he was thoroughly spoilt.

Chiago's heart sank when she heard this, and the fact that Pa Palagada had insisted on her helping him to bed did not make things easier for her. Pa Palagada liked her, that much she knew. By contrast, it would never have occurred to him that she might hate the very sight of him. He had insisted on her rubbing his back and cutting his nails, while he occasionally dipped his huge hands into her blouse. She had learned to stop protesting, to accept his attentions and be quiet about it all. But now they said this equally horrible son was coming from wherever they had dumped him for the past four years — was she to be used as a plaything for him too?

She had been mistaken in thinking that the other girls were all asleep. Ojebeta had not been quite sure whether the voices she was hearing were in a dream or reality; she soon found that it was real enough, when for the first time in a long while she discovered that their mat was damp. She moved on to the cool cemented floor. She was wide awake by the time Chiago was crying.

"I remember the last time," Chiago went on. "I was foolish in those days. I was bending down sweeping the floor when he came up behind me and jumped on me. He pulled at the small breasts I had then . . . I was not at all developed. . . . It hurt so, and I screamed. Do you know what he did? He slapped me hard on both sides of my face. I cried and told his mother, and was ordered to shut up. He must have told some story to his father, because for quite a long time he would cane me mercilessly for any little thing I did."

"That is very strange," Nwayinuzo countered. "We all think Pa Palagada has a kind eye for you."

"That's of recent," agreed Chiago. What she could not bring herself to tell her friend was that she had had to give in completely to the man's gross appetite. That each time their mistress had gone to another village to sell her abada cloth, Pa Palagada would call her to his room on any pretext. Many a time she had come out feeling physically ill and sick at heart; but at least he had promised her her freedom, and that he would one day make her his second wife. Things had been relatively easy for her since then. She sometimes wondered if Ma Palagada knew. But she was surprised that Nwayinuzo had noticed.

"Don't worry, you may not have to go to his son's room when he comes. After all, they have that black girl from Ibuza now. She's remotely related to Ma, you know. They may be reserving Ojebeta for him — perhaps they'll send her to keep their son amused," Nwayinuzo said by way of consolation, turning to face the wall in an attempt to catch up with some of her lost sleep.

At this statement, Chiago started to giggle. "Yes, that may be so — but she's very young, only ten."

Nwayinuzo turned round and laughed too. "Don't you know that if men start fiddling with a young girl it hastens her growth? That one is already going to be very tall too. But if both father and son want you, there'll be trouble in this household."

"Yes. I certainly don't want the father to feel that I like his son better than him. I don't like either of them. But what can I do. . . ."

"Yes," drawled Nwayinuzo sleepily, "but what can we do?"

They were quiet after this, and Ojebeta guessed that the two girls had dropped off to sleep. But their midnight conversation disconcerted her. She had heard rumours that Ma had a son, a very conceited man called something like "Kiriford", though she did not understand why Chiago should be so unhappy over his coming back. Neither did Ojebeta understand why they should mention her name like that.

In spite of it being over three years since she had come to this household, she had never stopped thinking of her home town, particularly when she was depressed or had been harshly treated. Whenever they went to Otu market, and she went to the waterside, she still used to gaze across the tangle of boats, canoes and steamers, across the River Niger, thinking to herself that one day she would cross over to her town a free person. She would go to her big mother Uteh's household and live with her. She knew she would be well received by her people, so endlessly elastic was the extended family system of the Ibuza people.

Now these two girls were talking of her being reserved for some horrible man, who might slap her on both sides of her face if she protested. Protested against what? The more she thought about their conversation, the more puzzled she was. What exactly were they talking about? She thought about Pa Palagada — he was not completely mad in the sense that he needed locking up, but he was a very intolerant master. The only method he knew of making those under him do as he wanted was by caning. If you did not look at him when he was talking to you, you got the cane. If you stared at him too much, you were caned. If you laughed at him, the same treatment applied; but if he cracked a joke and you did not laugh, you were caned. The man was crazy with power. If his son was like that, too, Ojebeta knew that life was going to be terrible for them all. It might be just tolerable having one crazy master, but two — God save them!

She tried eventually to sleep again, but she need not have bothered, for before she could snatch a few minutes big Jienuaka was ringing his bell for them to wake up.

"It can't be time yet," Ojebeta mumbled to her room mates who were just waking. "Even the cocks are still asleep."

"This is a special day," said Nwayinuzo in a sulky voice. "Ma's son Clifford is arriving from a town called Lagos today. We have to fetch more water than usual, we have to clean all the rooms in the house and sweep all the dirt from the yard. Because we alone will not be welcoming him; many people will be coming to see him too. He's been away for over three years."

They trooped down to the River Nkisi and, as if the young man coming was going to inspect every crevice of their bodies, they all bathed thoroughly. They returned, and went back several times, until every pot and every available water drum in the yard was filled with water. Then they swept the yard and Chiago, with Ojebeta to help her, went into one of the rooms at the extreme end of the big house, in the part that was seldom used unless there were guests staying.

"Make sure you sweep under that bed properly," said Chiago as she opened the wooden shutters on the windows to let in fresh air, "because Clifford likes complaining about very little things. And he's the apple of Ma's eye."

Ojebeta did as she was told, and then asked all of a sudden: "What is he like, this Clifford, Ma's son? Is he as wicked as Pa?"

"Who told you Pa is wicked? Get on with your job and stop spreading gossip. Can you imagine what this place would be like if there were no Pa? Would Ma be able to control giant slaves like Jienuaka by herself? Get on with your work!"

If Ojebeta detected a trace of unfamiliar loyalty to Pa in Chiago's words, she was not commenting on it. She had become wiser than her age, and knew when to keep quiet. Like the older girls who had been here longer, she had learned to accept life as a slave with little complaint; it might be rigorous or unfair, with no freedom of movement, but at least it provided them with food, clothing and shelter. Circumstances could have been worse.

Soon the whole Palagada household had an air of festivity and nervous expectancy. A fat pig had been killed earlier in the day by Jienuaka and the kitchen had been very busy. The girls were told to put on their best abadas, and Chiago had on a blouse made of velvet; no one knew why Ma had decided to let her wear this expensive material, and the others assumed that as usual the blouse was made from left-overs.

In the evening, when the sun was beginning to go down and the slaves and servants of the Palagada household had finished their day's work, they all sat on the veranda in the back yard, waiting for the arrival of the son of their mistress. The two males slaves had gone to the waterside to fetch the young master, to carry his baggage and to bring him home.

They waited for a long time, during which Amanna decided to play about on the stony ground in the yard. Chiago warned her several times to be careful about her new clothes, but Amanna would not do as she was told. She began to skip with an imaginary rope, apparently enjoying herself so much that she asked Ojebeta to join her and be her partner. The temptation was too great to be resisted, for they seldom had time to play at all, never had time to be the children that they really were. Peals of laughter rang from the two girls, and they completely forgot that they were so near the big house and that Pa could hear them.

He now came out, his belly protruding, the braces of his mighty trousers hanging loose so that he was obliged to hold the trousers up with one hand. He was sweating profusely as he thundered, "What do you think you two are doing, making so much noise that we cannot talk in the house? What, eh, what? Come up to the parlour — and, you, go and get me the whip. I will teach you two to laugh properly next time."

It was to Ijeoma that he had pointed his fat finger, and she scurried to the pantry where the canes were kept in order and brought out the special one reserved for the small girls. As they followed Pa into the parlour, Chiago looked at them with eyes that said, *Did I not tell you so?*

When they went in Pa Palagada started to ask them silly questions. He wanted to know why they had been playing, why they were so happy, laughing like "lunatics". Trying to shift the blame to each other, as most children in similar circumstances would, Ojebeta said it was Amanna who had started it, and Amanna said the noise had started when her friend joined her. The knowledge of an impending beating made them desperate.

Pa Palagada watched them with bloodshot eyes, looking from one to the other, as their accusations went backwards and forwards like a ball in a game. As the feelings of the two friends became more intense, he burst out laughing. Eventually the quarrel graduated to other areas.

"I saw you the other day, you little thief from Ibuza," said Amanna, "munching some dried fish on your way to the Nkisi stream. You stole that fish. I had nothing to do with that."

"It's a lie, it's a lie. You're just saying that so that Pa our master will cane me and not you. I did not steal any fish, and I did not make any noise just now. What about you, eh? It was you who ate the green mangoes near the church that other time. I saw you eating, and I reminded you that Ma had told us not to pick the green mangoes from the Catholic Fathers' gate. I saw you—"

She could not finish, for Amanna had pounced on her and the two girls began to fight. Pa Palagada moved his expensive green bottle of schnapps out of the way. He had been given a whole case of it, by one of the Dutch traders who worked for the United Africa Company, but he seldom drank any of it except on occasions like this, when his only son was coming home. The girls tore at each other until their clothes were in shreds. Soon Amanna let out a haunting cry of real pain, for Ojebeta had dug her teeth into her upper arm. With one big roaring laugh Pa started to lash them left, right and centre with the cane. All they could do was separate from each other and cower in the corner of the room crying hysterically.

Chiago and the others outside heard the girls' painful cries and their hearts ached for them, but there was nothing they could do. The anguished sounds came intermittently. The screams would go on for a few minutes, then they would stop, then begin again. What was happening was that Pa was urging Ojebeta and Amanna to fight. But something came over the two girls and they refused to fight. Pa pushed them together, facing each other, but they were both exhausted. He taunted them.

"Ojebeta, so you started all the noise and then stole some dried fish, eh?" He laughed in his riotous way, and took a drink from his green schnapps bottle.

Ojebeta said nothing, but hiccoughed in pain and covered her face with her arms just in case the cane was about to land on her for not answering.

Pa tried again, this time with Amanna. "So, you are so scared of the thief from Ibuza that you cried, eh?"

Amanna breathed hard. Her eyes were full of hatred, and it showed. She looked at their master and torturer with disgust, but said nothing.

Pa saw the look and did not like it. He made a dash for the girl, she dodged him, and the cane instead of hitting Amanna curled back and lashed his wrist. Pa roared like a mad lion — so terrible was his voice that the whole house seemed to shake. Ma Palagada, who had been in the bathroom washing and dressing herself in a special complete velvet outfit, waddled out, panic in her eyes. The servants and slaves forgot their manners and rushed into the parlour to see what the matter was. The sound of the girls receiving punishment was something they were used to, but this was different.

They saw Pa shouting in pain, and Ma rubbing some of the schnapps on his wrist, but they did not know what had happened and did not have the courage to ask.

Pa turned round and bellowed, "Clear out of here to your quarters, you good-for-nothing slaves!"

The picture the Palagadas presented was both noisy and ridiculous. Ma had only had time to tie her velvet lappa on top of her breasts; in fact she had been sure that the row was being caused by one of the male slaves butchering her husband (as some U.A.C.

Europeans had said some slaves were doing to their masters on some plantation farms). And Pa, his eyes red with both pain and anger now, was holding on to his wrist and still howling, *"Nnem-oooo . . . Nnemoo!"* He always cried for his mother whenever he had the slightest ailment, even if it was an ordinary minor touch of malaria. He was one of those big, manly males who would not hesitate to tell you that women were created as playthings for men, that they were brainless, mindless, and easily pliable. And yet it was to a woman that he would go to pour out his troubles, wanting her to listen, to sympathise and make appropriate noises, to give him a cuddle, tell him how handsome and kind he was, and how everything was going to be all right and that he should not worry. Yet he never respected any woman. Now here he was, calling upon his mother, long since dead, to come out of the grave and take away the stinging pain he had inflicted upon himself.

The group of slaves stood by the heavy damask curtains at the parlour door, watching their master behaving like a child; in opposite corners of the room stood Ojebeta and Amanna, now really frightened, not knowing what their fate would be. Pa thundered again and waved them all away with his other hand. Ojebeta and Amanna took to their heels. Ojebeta ran to a small bush at the back of the yard, where she decided to stay and observe how things went; if it came to the very worst, she could try to run away again. Amanna, on the other hand, was too distraught to run anywhere. She simply went to their sleeping room and wept, not minding Ijeoma's warning that she would be needed to be shown to Clifford when he arrived.

Ojebeta in her hiding place thought of so many things. She did not cry, though she felt really sorry for herself and for her friend Amanna, who was in greater pain than she was. She determined that one day she would have her revenge on the horrid man. She had seen that Pa Palagada felt pain even more than they who had become accustomed to whipping. Just one lash on the wrist, and see all the fuss he was making! She wished Jienuaka could be persuaded to whip him one day, just to show him; even though she could not see how that could ever happen, the thought of it made her glad.

Eventually she heard the excitement and happy laughter of her mistress, and the counterfeited cheer of the slaves, and knew that her services would soon be required. If she did not come out of hiding, there would be another excuse for a caning from Pa Palagada.

Her best blouse was torn so she had to go to their sleeping-room to get her house blouse; after all, it was getting dark and there were so many people for Ma's son to see. She could not care less whether or not he approved of how she looked. Inside the room she saw her friend Amanna still weeping and pitying herself, and her heart went out to her.

"It wasn't my fault that we had to fight, you know," she apologised. "I really didn't want to fight you. You know that you're my best friend and the only friend I have . . . and that horrid man made me fight you. My dead parents would burn him for ever and ever."

She sat by Amanna, and they both swore that they would always be friends, that they would never again betray one another just to amuse Pa. Then they heard Ijeoma calling and they knew it was time for them to be shown, like fatted cows, to their master's son Clifford.

He was a tall man, very black like Pa; in fact he was the very image of Pa but for the fact that he was thinner than his father. He also had a very black moustache, unlike his father, which joined with a sparse beard he was apparently just cultivating; the latter was beginning to hide his otherwise hollow cheeks. He looked starved, and older than his years. His eyes were mischievous, like his father's; one could not yet tell whether they too were incapable of kindness.

"They are all well fed and well clothed," he approved, glancing perfunctorily at the line of people in front of him. He had no special salutation for anyone, not even Chiago whom he had known so well. He simply asked in passing if the black girl with tribal marks on her face was from Ibuza, and his mother said, yes, she came from her people.

He walked past them, arrogant in his dark trousers, white shirt and black bowtie, strode into the dining apartment of the big house, where Jienuaka and Chiago had to follow to serve the family and their guests. Ojebeta and the others had to go to the kitchen to help the chief cook, another Onitsha woman, who would be extremely cross if none of the girls were around to help her fetch and carry water. She was not a slave but a widow, in Ma's employment.

She made sure everyone knew this.

9 A Rich Religion

Ma Palagada's son did not turn out after all to be as bad as Ojebeta had been led to expect. At least he did not treat them roughly physically. Yes, he ordered everyone about, wanting this and wanting that, even when the things he demanded were within his own reach. But that was the behaviour of people brought up in big houses where there were many servants and slaves. For, they told themselves, if they had to bother to tie their own shoelaces and cut their fingernails themselves, what were the slaves and servants for?

One evening when the girls were busy in the kitchen, they saw the Palagads seeing off a white woman. It was Ijeoma who saw them first and called to the others.

"Come, everybody, come and see Ma and Pa talking to an *oyibo!*"

Of course they all ran out, including the big Jienuaka. He left the wood he was breaking for the fire, dropped his axe and went to the gate leading out of the backyard, where he could watch with the others unseen. They were not the only ones fascinated by the sight. Many children from up and down the narrow street came out, following the "oyibo" in a crowd a little distance from her. A few of the local people, especially those who traded with the foreigners at Otu market, had seen red-faced men, who were suppoesd to be white. Those men, however, seldom brought their wives with them. They usually made do with local girls, giving them babies and leaving them; that was why places near the sea, such as Sapele, Onitsha and Warri, were full of so many "half-castes". But here was a white woman, a rare sight.

"I wonder how Ma understands what she says," mused Ojebeta, as they all pressed against each other to get a better glimpse of this strange person.

"Ma does not understand, but Clifford does. Besides they say

the woman *oyibo* speaks a kind of Ibo. You have to listen very carefully to understand it — she speaks through her nose, and pro-
nounces her words in a funny way," Jienuaka volunteered, breathing heavily as he was wont.

There was a gentle ripple of laughter among them, the kind of
laughter that can be identified with suppressed making fun of over-
lords and supposed "betters".

Encouraged by their mutual mischievous joy, Ijeoma remarked,
"How starved she looks! See how her hips are flat and shapeless,
as if she was a lizard lying flat on its stomach. She must be ill all the
time."

"Perhaps that is why they don't bring their wives to these shores,
and instead make our girls have children the colour of unripe palm
fruits."

They all laughed again and someone, probably Chiago, wondered
if a woman as thin and ill-looking as that could ever bear children
of her own.

Nobody replied to that, for now Jienuaka called them to go back
to their duties. Even in this short minute of freedom, the slave
mentality was still dominant in him. Jienuaka was the type who,
although he could enjoy a joke, would never be disloyal to his
master. It never occurred to any of them, not even the other male
servants, to say "no" to Jienuaka, for he was such a formidably big
person, so tall, so broad of shoulder and so strong that his nickname — "Agwuele" — meant a giant.

Within a few days they knew, or suspected, why the weak-looking
white woman had paid them a visit. Her husband was the new
United Africa Company chief, and she helped to run the local
Church Missionary Society school. She wanted Ma Palagada to
send some of her children there. However, whereas people then
were still very reluctant to consign their actual children to these
foreign places of learning, it was acceptable to send domestic slaves
so long as their going did not tamper with their daily tasks. Ma
Palagada could not spare her girls on weekdays, or on market days;
but the day called Sunday came only once in seven. She did not mind
that, especially as the white woman, Mrs Simpson, said that on
Sundays the girls would only stay for a few hours after church.

For the girls it was a great excitement. They had new outfits
made for them in plain materials, outfits that did not have separate
tops and lappas but were all joined together — what Mrs Simpson
called a gown and the girls called "gam". They were quite shape-

102

less, with puffed sleeves. The girls were also made to wear some hats, tied on to their heads with cloth round the sides. In church they were taught that women's heads were holy and should be covered.

More market stalls were assigned to Ma Palagada as an indirect result of this, and because of her connections she could buy any import at wholesale price before her rivals had time to do so. So she became doubly rich. Seeing that conversion from nothing to Christianity brought Ma financial rewards, a number of smaller traders followed suit, and when the "nobodies" saw that the rich were all going to this new place called church, many were converted to this fashionable religion.

It was with this great enthusiasm that the first Christ Church Cathedral was built. Church-going every morning became a feature of the Palagada home, and Ma was regarded everywhere as an enviable and god-fearing woman.

"Does she not drink tea in the afternoon? Does she not wear 'gam' every Sunday?" her neighbours asked.

However, even under the influence and tuition of this Mrs Simpson, it was difficult for Ma Palagada and her society women contemporaries to go completely European. There was no problem about wearing the straight-shaped English dresses, even with their overfed stomachs; but then they would add the type of heavy headtie that went with native lappas, and they would also place an extra piece of material on their shoulders, regardless of whether the English lady thought it appropriate. This was because the Ibo belief was that a complete woman must have two lappas round her waist, not just one. You might sometimes put the second piece of cloth over your shoulders, but you must be seen to use both as befitted a properly married woman: so Ma Palagada and her group did not wish to be thought of with disrespect. The correctness of what they felt seemed to be confirmed for them when one day, during the regular Wednesday women's class meeting that had been established, Mrs Simpson showed them a picture of the woman she said had ruled England. The women gasped at her size.

"Look, no wonder she had many children like us. She was well fed," Ma Palagada remarked in an aside to her friend Ma Mee.

"And look, she has her *ntukwasi* over her shoulder."

"Why then does this one Mrs Simpson wear so few clothes, when she ought to dress to look respectable?"

Ma Mee in her newly converted attitude knew that it was a sin

103

to backbite — did not the Bible say it was like killing your neighbour? — so she asked the Englishwoman direct: "Why do you not dress like your queen?"

Mrs Simpson, who in her heart of hearts regarded these women as having the brains of children, said patiently, "Because it is too hot for me here. The queen wore more clothes and in darker colours because in my country it can be so cold that dew and rain form themselves into snow. Also her husband had died when this picture was taken." Then she had to go into a great lengthy explanation to describe what "snow" meant, for none of these women in their wildest imagination could think of what it might be. Nonetheless she managed to convey to them the fact that snow was white, and that it was formed from water; it would be essential that they understood when they came across the simile "as white as snow" in their Ibo-translated Bibles.

As far as Ma Palagada's girls were concerned, this new religion they learned once a week was the greatest thing to happen to them — getting ready for church and then, later in the day, the Sunday school they called "Akwukwo-Uka". Ojebeta would never forget the first church harvest festival she experienced. Weeks before Ma had bought them all new material, and in order that they would learn how to sew she made them make their own clothes. Chiago was now an expert in sewing. Before they started going to Akwukwo-Uka, she would simply look at you and guess your measurements, and would then proceed to make the blouse or whatever it was you wanted. But she had since learned to count and use her tape rule. Ojebeta and the others could not make a "gam" or full dresses yet, though after Chiago had done the cutting they would have to stitch them all over again.

Intrigued, Ojebeta had one day asked Chiago: "Why is it that first you get a nice piece of material — a perfect piece, which you ought to just throw over your body exactly as it is — and what you do then is to tear it into pieces. But then you start sewing the pieces back together again. It doesn't make sense."

Chiago had to think for some time before she answered, for she saw Ojebeta's point of view. "If you don't cut the cloth into pieces and then stitch them together, the dress would have no shape, and we would have no work to do in the market. We would just be sitting about doing nothing, and that would be no good to anybody, especially us. You see, we make things for outsiders and they pay our Ma, and that helps her to feed and clothe us."

104

On the latter point Chiago was quite wrong; for the amount of money the girls made for Ma from sewing alone was enough to keep the household going. In allowing her girls to go to Mrs Simpson's classes, she had allowed them to become élite slaves. They soon learned to read in Ibo from a green book called *Azu-Ndu*, and what they found out from the printed word gave them endless amusement; they read and re-read the stories, the sayings, until they knew most of the little book off by heart. So it was to Ma's stalls that people brought their material to be made into the type of gown that the white woman wore, because there you were properly measured and the girls who sewed could read from books. It was because of this attitude of customers that Ma's son Clifford, who was becoming very interested in his mother's business, advised her to increase her charges. She did this, and their profit and prestige went up even higher, for the people of Otu Onitsha, true to human nature, valued more what they paid dearly for. It seemed that every woman wanted to be able to say, "I am not a pagan, I go to church, and my church 'gam' was made for me at the Palagada stalls in Otu Onitsha."

The girls were busier than ever as the first church harvest approached. Many of the successful people who had made a great deal of money from selling palm kernels instead of slaves were converted to some form of Christianity, which meant that they all wanted to wear some new outfit for the harvest festival. The girls were encouraged to work even harder by the expectation that they too would have something new to wear, for they knew that Ma Palagada liked to plan little surprises even for her lowliest servant.

It happened on one market day. Ma, after settling them all to their different jobs, called casually:

"Ojebeta, Ijeoma, come with me to the shore; a big steamer is coming in from the port."

"Yessima." (This was one of the first lessons you learned as a servant or slave, that when you were called by any lady, you did not answer "Eh!" as you would do in your village; you were meant to reply, "Ma'am" — which usually came out sounding more like a goat crying for food. To men you said "Sa!" So in privileged houses the refrain was Ma, Sa, Sa, Ma, all day.)

The girls left the work they were supposed to be doing and stood almost to attention, ready for Ma's next orders. That they were going to the shore was in itself an excitement; Ojebeta loved watching those steamers and launches and canoes coming to the bank of

105

the river. Having given Chiago some final instructions and warned her to tie every penny she made securely in her waist belt, Ma said to the two impatiently waiting girls, "Let us go."

At the riverside that day Ojebeta had never seen so many white men together. They had red faces and were dressed alike, with small white hats on their heads. They all seemed to walk with a swagger. They were very noisy and happy, and flirted with some of the girls who had come with their owners to collect goods from the big boats. One white man even slapped Ojebeta on the back, and when she turned to look at him he winked at her, which made his red face under his yellow hair look quite comical.

Ma was allowed inside one of the big boats, while they stood at the waterside. After they had waited for what seemed ages, a young sailor came out of the boat carrying a huge bale of light blue material on his shoulder. Ma was carrying a square case of something, and the girls rushed forward eagerly to relieve her of it. Ijeoma was asked to take the bale of cloth from the sailor, and as the heavy bale was placed on her head Ijeoma's neck shrank a little under the weight.

On their way back to the stall they hardly stopped at all. After they had arrived, and Ma had been given a bowl of the day's palm wine, she asked Chiago:

"Do you still have a large number of dresses to cut and sew?"

"Yessima — because of the harvest festival. I don't know whether we shall be able to finish them all in time, for there are only three market days left. Maybe some of the people will let me take the work home, then we can finish them for the next market."

Ma thought about this, knowing that their household duties would suffer if the girls were to take market sewing home. She knew also that her husband, who she had long suspected had an eye for the big girl Chiago, would be furious. He liked the girls to be free to attend to his every needs whenever he called them. On the other hand, Ma knew that it would be a good plan if in the future Chiago and one or two of the other girls could stay at home to sew. And if there was too much work, she would have to look around and see if she could buy or employ another girl. She preferred to buy one, though, for then you owned the complete person.

"That will have to be something for the future, because you are all going to be very busy now, making your own harvest gowns."

The hush and expectancy that followed this statement was almost tangible. Amanna opened her mouth wide, and Nwayinuzo stopped

106

what she was doing and gazed attentively at her mistress.

"Yes, you will be using that bale of blue muslin for your dresses. You will make them in the latest fashion, not the ordinary styles you have been making for other people. Make them special, like those of the European ladies. They should be long, with frills on the bottom and lace on the sleeves. We shall see that you all look very nice. . . ."

The girls' eyes were now as round as ripe red palm fruits. Amanna had to cover her mouth to prevent herself from shouting out with joy. They were really going to look like real ladies! As for Ojebeta, she felt like dancing round this remarkable fat lady in appreciation of her kindness — it was at times like this that she felt grateful for having been bought by her.

Of course she still longed constantly to go home, for Ibuza was like something permanently in your bloodstream. She had felt a little strange that very morning when she had seen some of her people arriving from their villages in cheap canoes, shouting instead of talking, and badly dressed, struggling with their tins of palm oil. They did not know her: Ibuza as a whole was quite a large place; but the marks on her face would have identified her to them as coming from one of the Western Ibo towns, even if they could not be sure which one. She knew that the issue would be further complicated when she spoke. Gone was her abrasive Ibuza accent; she now spoke like a girl born in Onitsha, with rounded "Rs" and a slowness of delivery, each word drawn out.

But at times like these, it was as if she hardly even cared whether she ever went back or not. Her small, square, white basket — Ma had bought one for each of them — was almost full of clothes. She had enough to eat, and she went to Sunday School. The harsher aspects of being a Palagada slave girl receded temporarily. Waking up from her musings, she joined the others in their gratitude.

"Thank you, Ma, for being so kind to us. May God make you prosper the more."

Chiago hesitantly went forward to feel the material.

"It's very soft, like a baby's skin, and shiny, too," she remarked. "I like it very much."

The others crowded round, in turn touching and admiring, with broad smiles on their faces. On closer inspection they saw that some careless person had spilt a yellowish liquid on part of the beautiful cloth; but they all agreed with Chiago that it was the best material they had seen produced by the Europeans.

107

"It is called 'Mossulu', that is why," Amanna explained.

Once more the others agreed. Then Ma said, in a voice that signalled it was time to return to their work:

"There will be enough for everybody, even when you cut off the soiled part."

"Yessima, there will be more than enough."

Ma Palagada felt quite pleased with herself. She had ordered the muslin to cover some straight-backed chairs she and her husband had bought from the U.A.C. people some time before. But some of the sailors had poured some drink on the bale and it had soaked through. They had promised to bring her a perfect, unsoiled one on their next trip. Meanwhile she had offered to take this one off their hands, since it was of no use to them. She knew it would make nice church outfits for her girls.

The night before the harvest festival the Palagada girls, with girls from other houses, went to the church to polish the new pews and shine the floors.

Many farmers from neighbouring villages had brought their fattest yams and hens and goats and bananas and plantains, and everything they had which was eatable, and had sold them to the rich who could then give them as harvest offerings to God. Ma Palagada was not one to be left behind that harvest year. On the night before the big day, her compound was filled with all kinds of vegetables, all kinds of animals — from sheep to pigeons, all making their different animal sounds, so that anyone entering the compound could be forgiven for believing they were in another "Noah's Ark" like the one written about in the Christian Bible.

The hurry and bustle of that Sunday morning was unprecedented. Ma Palagada was adorned in pure velvet, all lustrous and blue, with rows and rows of coral beads laced with gold around her neck. Pa was dressed in a white *popo* cloth, a dazzling white European shirt, and a felt cap with embroidery worked all over it and a feather — the mark of his newly acquired title — sticking out of it. He too had rows of long coral beads round his neck. He wore a pair of hand-made slippers, sewn in the Gold Coast, which were shaped like fishes, with golden thread running through them and pieces of gold stitched in between the toes. He carried a mighty fan that was made in the same way as the slippers. He looked really magnificent and he knew it, for he held himself upright and was even sober, a rare state for him those days.

When there was only about an hour to go, and the church bells were pealing their bell songs. Ma in her velvet costume came to where the girls were busy admiring themselves and told them to tie the legs of the hens and the cocks, arrange the yams and plantains, put a rope round the goats, and then go round the neighbourhood singing *"Kai sua ani . . ."* — "We plant the field and scatter. . . ."

"So that the pagans will know how blessed we are," she said. She thought to herself that this might even convert some to their brand of Christianity.

"Yessima," the girls chorused, delighted.

They quickly collected the harvest offerings together and arranged them in big enamel bowls, the type of bowls basically made to serve as baths but which many people then found useful for carrying heavy foodstuff. The fowls the girls carried on their heads, lifting their muslin dresses clear of the ground with one hand; the male servants and slaves led the bigger animals by ropes, and they all went round the streets singing Ibo versions of harvest songs.

It was an impressive sight that they made. People ran out of their huts and houses to watch, to marvel at how beautiful, how rich these people were. Why, the servants were even dressed in silk!

Ojebeta and Amanna were in front, carrying two hens each (the hens in Amanna's bowl protested throughout the procession, flapping their wings in anger, and making their bearer sing out of tune many a time). They were followed by the bigger girls, and then the men. One of the most striking sights was Jienuaka. He was dressed in close-fitting trousers given to him by Clifford, trousers that were so tight that they clung everywhere to the shape of his anatomy. His shirt, which Chiago had made, had ruffles like those on the girls' dresses; and he sported a broad-brimmed hat made of straw, and old cloth shoes which in their better days Pa had used as bedroom slippers. And Jienuaka was leading the fattest and the strongest goat. He could not, however, join in the songs, for he did not know them and they sounded to him very strange. He still found it difficult to master the Ibo alphabet; but his master did not very much need that ability in him so no one minded.

After they had gone round their neighbourhood twice, and the final church bell was pealing, they returned to the front of their house and waited for the Palagadas. And they soon came out in style, all the members of the family. Pa and Ma walked with dignity and Clifford with a youthful swagger. Those who watched them envied and admired them, the "Church Missionary Society" Christians.

No one actually knew whether this type of display managed to bring many pagans to Christ; what was apparent was that in many Ibo towns the wealthy and successful people were usually members of the Church of England. The masses, on the other hand, tended to become Roman Catholics.

By the time Ojebeta and her fellow slaves and servants had taken their places at the back of the church, they were already tired. She did not much listen to the sermons and the readings, but she sang joyfully to all the new church tunes she had learned from the white woman at Sunday School. Though they had been provided with some Ibo hymn books, they did not need them for they knew all the words by heart.

Amid loud singing and jubilant music, the white man who was wearing a black robe and was known as the Bishop called: "The Palagadas!"

At first none of the household realised that it was them he was calling; the way he said the *P* instead of *kP* as it should be pronounced made it sound strange. After he had repeated the name several times Ma recognised that he was referring to them. She stood up in all her majesty, walked down the aisle to the back seats where her household was sitting — amidst the admiring glances which she was very aware were following her progress — and made frantic signs for them to come up. It took quite a while to wake Jienuaka, but at last, with all the hens, goats and everything else, they went up to the front of the altar. The Bishop took the gifts from them, blessed the labour of their hands, and told them to obey their masters and work diligently in all they were employed to do. And he begged God to accept the offerings of his subjects.

The whole church, having stopped singing, said "Amen", in voices deep with reverence.

The slaves and servants, happy to have been blessed, walked back to their designated places at the back of the church, away from their superiors, and sang more songs.

10 Signs of Change

When, in later years, Ojebeta looked back to that time, she could only remember that after that first and happy church harvest things began to change rather rapidly. It was at this time that she learned that nothing lasts for ever, that people must come and they must go.

The first sign of change was Ma Palagada's sudden illness. Ojebeta did not know how it had all started. One day everything about their routine was as trouble-free as usual: going to the market, sewing, selling, Ma holding conferences with various traders, black and white. The next day their stalls in Otu were not opened at all, because Ma was so ill.

From their part of the compound the girls saw different doctors, mostly native ones, coming and going; and Ma still did not get better. Chiago and Ijeoma, both of them now grown young women, took it in turns to sleep in Ma's bedroom, for she had to be fed on a special light pap and her chamber-pot needed attending to. So the hard work of nursing her fell on them.

The other girls went to Ma's room every morning to wish her good morning, and enquire how she was, and tell her that they were hoping and praying to God that she would be better soon.

"Do you really want her to get well?" Amanna, still mischievous, asked Ojebeta after Ma had been laid up for two market days running.

"I do, I really do." And she meant it. For now, nearly eight years after she had left her village, Ojebeta had started to ask herself some questions. If her own people really cared for her, could they not at least enquire about what had become of her and where she was staying? No, she did not want anything bad to happen to Ma, for she had not yet made up her mind about whether she still wanted to go back to Ibuza after all.

"If anything happens to Ma," Amanna said, half to herself and

111

half to Ojebeta. "I will probably have to go and live with her daughter in Bonny, until I get married to someone."

"That would be terrible, being sent to live with Ma's daughter in Bonny. And who is going to marry you — have you got your eye on someone?" Ojebeta asked, wanting to laugh.

"Have you ever seen a woman who never got a husband?" countered Amanna.

It did not need a reply. Every woman, whether slave or free, must marry. All her life a woman always belonged to some male. At birth you were owned by your people, and when you were sold you belonged to a new master, when you grew up your new master who had paid something for you would control you. It was a known fact that although Ma Palagada was the one who had bought them, they ultimately belonged to Pa Palagada, and whatever he said or ordered would hold.

Suddenly Amanna puffed, and rose from the crouching position she had been in all afternoon peeling cassava. "Do you know what Ijeoma said to me yesterday?"

Ojebeta looked up, none too happy; the unanswered question of what would happen to her was becoming predominant in her thoughts. "What did she say?" she dutifully asked her friend, knowing full well that she would eventually be told anyway, whether she wanted to hear or not.

"Ijeoma overheard them in the big house saying that if this new native doctor doesn't make Ma better, her eldest daughter Victoria will be coming to stay here to help her get healthy again."

"Well, after all, she is her daughter," Ojebeta replied philosophically. "She has to be near her mother in case anything should happen. But I feel it in my bones that nothing bad is going to happen to our Ma."

"She will die, one day."

"And so will you, you witch!"

Ma Palagada in her younger days had been "kept" by a Portuguese man who had been very kind to her. Though she never officially married him, this white man would always stay with her whenever his steam brought him to the banks of the Niger. The two daughters Ma had by this man she gave the English names of Victoria and Elizabeth. Much later, however, the man had to go because his people's trade — mainly slavery — was squeezed out. But he left Ma a great deal of wealth: coral beads, earrings, some silver and some copper-plated, cases and cases of gin and schnapps, bales of cloth and lots of money. It was at this time that Ma began to trade at Otu market. Her daughters, consequently, knew nothing about poverty. They knew that one could buy slaves, or have house servants and treat them even worse than slaves, for at that time just to keep another person from hunger was in itself felt to be payment enough. They had never considered that slaves and servants were human like themselves. Victoria showed a gentle disposition towards people she regarded to be of her own class, but she would take "no nonsense" from any menials; whenever she came to visit her mother the sting of her canes and her incessant slaps were widely felt. Now that she was married, to a school headmaster in Bonny, and had daughters of her own she was even more vicious, just like a bitch with puppies.

Ma did not improve, and within a few days Victoria and her two small daughters had come to Otu Onitsha and installed themselves in the Palagada home. Ojebeta was given the special task of looking after the children. They were lovely little girls with pale skin like that of their mother. The deep brown colour of their hair never stopped fascinating Ojebeta. As for their mother, superficially, at least, she was remarkably beautiful, even taller than Ma and with skin like that of young coffee beans and silky dark brown hair.

The very first night she arrived she told Ojebeta: "You must have your bath twice a day — night and morning — and you will no longer sleep in the common room in the back yard but in the corridor in front of our bedroom door, in case the children want to use the toilet at night." So, for the first time in eight years, Ojebeta was separated from her friends and companions.

She was kept busy all day looking after Victoria and the children, endlessly washing their clothes, taking them out to different places, playing with them, begging them to eat up their food, and she now seldom had time to see the other girls. The work was so copious and the demand so frequent that Ojebeta began to lose weight and was becoming more apathetic. One evening when she was feeding the youngest child, the other called her to fetch a drink of water. No sooner had she gone to attend to the latter girl than the two-year-old turned her china plate upside down on her own head and promptly started to laugh. It was so funny that Ojebeta found herself smiling too, and unfortunately at that precise instant Clifford and his half-sister came in, both looking sad and worried. They had apparently come from their mother's room.

"What is going on here?" Miss Victoria exclaimed shrilly. "Look at my babies! Look at what this slave is doing to them! Take that—" she struck out at Ojebeta — "and that, and that! Oh, my God . . . what will I tell their father?"

Ojebeta was by this time seeing stars. She was too stunned to cry, and in her instinctive attempt to protect her face from the slappings of this irate young woman she let drop one of the children's china bowls which she had been holding. Of course the bowl broke into innumerable pieces, and this unleashed the very devil in Miss Victoria. She pounced on Ojebeta, hitting, pulling, spitting at her, and intermittently hissing,

"You good-for-nothing slave! You bush slave!"

"You must stop now, Victoria, I say *stop*. . . ."

Ojebeta turned to look at Clifford; his face was twisted in anger and his voice was menacingly low. His sister too was taken aback, too surprised at the seriousness in Clifford's voice to say anything. Then she recollected herself, and shouted at him:

"Why, she's only a slave! What is she to you?"

As Victoria made this statement, Ojebeta scrambled up from her crouching position, and suddenly what Clifford could see was not a slave but a person. In fact, not just an ordinary person but a girl with very dark skin, so shiny that it seemed freshly polished by some invisible hands, a young girl who still had the slight plumpness of childhood about her. Her face was round, her eyes, now strewn with tears, were a very deep brown and were fringed with thick dark lashes as if she had lined them with black *otangele*. He could see that she was also really quite developed, for his sister in her madness had torn part of Ojebeta's blouse, exposing the top of her small, firm breasts, breasts which now heaved in apprehension and anger.

Victoria watched his appraising eyes, and muttered as she made her way out of the room, "She's only a slave — I don't care what you think."

"But she is our relation, too."

"Who wants a relation like this — a poor one, who had to be sold by her people?" Victoria taunted from the corridor before making her way to her bedroom.

Ojebeta had by now grown accustomed to physical pain, and to the mental anguish of being disparaged as a slave by all and sundry; but seldom had people reminded her in so many words that she had been sold here by her own brother. She had tried to defend Okolie

114

in her mind: he had undoubtedly done what he did to save her from dying from starvation . . . though surely he could at least have come to visit her to see how she was faring with these people. He had not asked of her, he had not sent her any message. Neither had her other brother who left home before their mother died. Tears welled up in her eyes and she let them fall.

"Stop crying, and go and wash your face." Clifford's voice cut into her thoughts.

"The children — who will take care of them?" Ojebeta asked, like any oppressed person who when given a minute of freedom does not at first know what to do with it.

"I will take them to their mother. They are not hungry."

Ojebeta went to the back of the house and sat at the foot of the lemon tree. It provided a little shade, and the small plants growing wild under the tree, though they were not very tall, were enough to give one a bit of protection. She flung herself on the cool leaves and felt at peace. It was nearing evening and the glare of the sun had abated. A light breeze from the River Niger was fanning the whole area. She did not think, she did not worry. She did not even cry, but just lay there, eyes closed.

She must have fallen asleep, for she did not hear the footsteps of someone approaching very quietly, as if making a great effort to avoid waking a sleeping child. Clifford had watched Ojebeta leave the big house, had followed her with his eyes, looking out of the big window that opened on to the yard. It would never have occurred to him that his new interest in her might simply be prompted by pity, or even in some way by guilt. A sad girl, strong, healthy and almost beautiful. It was a shame her people had put all those strange patterns on her face; but no matter, she had perfect carriage and would grow into a proud-looking woman. Not just any woman, either, he told himself, beginning to explore and develop the idea forming in his mind: in these changing times an Ibo woman who could sew, cook and serve civilised food, even read and write her name, was going to be an asset to her husband. No, Ojebeta could not be considered an ordinary slave girl, particularly since they were related. Slavery was dying anyway; most of the slave markets he had known as a boy had now been closed. He walked close to Ojebeta and stood looking down at her, coiled there like a worm. She must have been really exhausted to be able to go into such a deep sleep in such an uncomfortable place.

He had an impulse to wake her and talk with her, though he

was uncertain what he would say. He coughed tentatively, and she quickly sprang up, as if she had not been asleep at all. She gasped, feeling guilty at being found thus, sleeping in the day when she ought to have been working.

Unexpectedly Clifford smiled and said in a voice strange to her — for it was many, many years since she had been spoken to in this mock teasing way — "I caught you out. What are you going to do about it?"

Ojebeta opened her mouth and closed it again. Her mind was racing ahead of her. What was this? Had he come here to beat her again, where his sister had left off? Her eyes wandered from side to side, like those of a trapped animal, and she prayed to God to please help her.

To some extent, things were difficult for Clifford as well, though he was a grown man of twenty-six — almost twice Ojebeta's age — and he was not unaware of his inadequacies. He had been sent originally to Lagos to gain a foothold in the new European work; however, he had preferred to return home and help in his mother's business. His father had resented this, saying that it was only foolish people who put all their eggs in one basket, and urging Clifford to try something else. But he was content to remain an Otu trader, keeping accounts and doing the physical travelling for his parents. Though he was a success at this, inside himself he still felt a failure, since he had been given the opportunity to branch out on his own yet had been unable to stand on his own feet. In a way it had all helped him to become a better person, a gentler and more considerate man — no longer the type of youth he had been a few years before, who had told Chiago to strip herself naked so that he might see what she had hidden between her legs. He now regretted his past behaviour. When in the privacy of his room he recalled the shameful things he used to do to some of their female slaves and servants he despised himself. This self-torture and self-examination had become even more painful now that he was a practising Christian.

His mother's illness was an additional problem. She might be just a woman like every other mother, but what a woman! It would be true to say that in fact it was she who owned all the family's wealth, but who would dare voice such an opinion when his drunkard of a father with his bulging stomach was there telling everyone, "Palagada is my wife, don't you forget that."

With all that on one's mind, how could one come to a slave girl in one's household and say, "Will you share my life with me?"

116

Clifford was at a loss as to how to broach the suggestion, though he had fully convinced himself that he could do worse than make her his wife.

Then Ojebeta said, "I would like to go and see how the children are. Miss Victoria will be furious." She started to make her way out of the little bush, avoiding as much as she possibly could any personal contact with Clifford.

But he felt it was one of those golden opportunities that must not be allowed to pass. He did not command her verbally, knowing very well that he could; he could have made her do anything, but that did not occur to him. He restricted her slightly, held her upper arm gently, yet firmly enough for her to get the message.

He was saying something; Ojebeta's mind could not focus and seemed to be flapping up and down like the tail of a fish out of water.

"You must not think of yourself as a slave like the other girls, you know. Because you may have to stay with me. Would you like that? Mother would like it."

Clifford was being very courteous, and that was the most he could humble himself to make Ojebeta realise how he was beginning to feel about her. One did not go to a slave one cared for and say straightaway, "I love you, I cannot live without you". That would be dramatising the issue, and showing more weakness than courage.

"Me?" Ojebeta asked, placing her hand on her chest. There seemed only one possible interpretation of his attentions. "Of course I will work for you if you want me to." She felt like adding, *Rather than your bad-tempered and spoilt sister Victoria*, though she refrained. What choice did she have anyway?

Clifford smiled slightly again and nodded, still holding her, now by the wrist. "Not just work for me, but to live with me. Or don't you want me to make you my wife when you grow up, in a year or two?"

"Me?" Ojebeta asked again stupidly. Then she said, "But I am only your mother's slave."

"Have you never heard of masters marrying their female slaves, then?"

Yes, Ojebeta had heard. Was that not one of the dreams older slave girls had, that their masters would find them attractive and make them if not a wife then a mistress, so that their housework was lessened and they were given an easier time on the whole? Ojebeta did not wish to ask the reason for this sudden change of

117

heart or question what had precipitated this move. She knew she was even lucky to have been warned at all. So she answered politely, saying what seemed the expected thing, not knowing whether she actually should feel glad or unhappy.

"I would love that. Thank you very much for wanting me. May I now go and look after the children?"

"Yes," Clifford said, frowning and letting go of her hand. "My sister will want you. But keep this in your mind, and do not tell anybody, until Ma gets better. Then I shall tell her and Pa." He knew his parents would prefer as a daughter-in-law one of those pale-skinned girls left on the shores of the Niger by their wandering white fathers, especially as most of them had some kind of wealth; but he would rather have an innocent girl, a girl who would forever look up to him. True, his mother had paid for her, though against that could be set the fact that she was a distant cousin. She would need polishing up for a year or so, then she would be ready for him.

"Ojebeta!" he called, using his masterly tone. "Tell nobody about this, until the time becomes ripe."

She turned round and nodded, a nod that implied: "My lips are sealed."

Ma was not getting better, so Victoria arranged for her to be taken to the newly opened hospital at Iyienu, a small town just then developing, a few miles from Onitsha. The advantage of Ma being there was that she was in the care of missionary nurses and once in a while she was visited by a proper white doctor who did all he could for her. This careful nursing, combined with the fact that she was away from her business worries and from the increasing anxiety over Pa Palagada's loose behaviour, helped improve her condition, though she had to stay a whole three more market days.

During this time her daughter indeed proved her worth and everyone praised her efforts. She must truly have loved her mother. She went to the hospital every evening and while there supervised the food prepared for Ma, for the hospital did not provide the patients' meals. Ijeoma had to stay there with Ma, cooking for her, and Miss Victoria came each evening to see that things were in order. Everyone was so busy running about helter-skelter that there was no one to go and run the market stalls. And this, they all knew, would deplete the family income.

On one of the few days when Pa Palagada had gone to Iyienu to see his wife, he came home pleased that she was recuperating faster than any of them had expected (though within himself he suspected that it would be a very long while before Ma was her old self again after this illness) and he told Chiago to call Clifford for him.

"I have been wanting to talk with you, Clifford," he began, then went straight to the point. "Many young people now go direct into business. It is only in Otu Onitsha that people think that trading in lappa material is women's work. Did you see that fellow Nwoba on the other side of Otu — he is from Emekuku: he now sews women's clothes. If we are not careful, all your mother's trade and customers will be taken over by other people. They are all wolves praying for her to die."

"No, she won't die yet, she will live to be old."

"That is our prayer; but at least some of her stalls must be kept going. Even if she dies — which we do not pray for, you and I, and all who love her — those she leaves behind must eat, mustn't we?"

"I will keep one of the stalls going," Clifford said slowly, "to start with, and use that as a base while I collect money from all those who owe her, for I am quite sure they are many. I keep a list of them. Amanna will have to help in fetching and carrying in the market. Ojebeta as you know looks after Victoria's children. Chiago will take up the sewing—"

"No!" It was like a dog barking, so forceful and full of anger. "Why must it be Chiago all the time? The poor girl is overworked. Why can't the others learn to sew? Why must it be just that girl . . . ?"

Pa Palagada was surprised at himself, at his tactless outburst. Clifford did not know what to say. He had always doubted that Chiago's long stays in his father's bedroom were merely to tidy his bed and cut his nails. But nobody had said anything, and he had allowed sleeping dogs to lie. Now, he felt a stab in his heart as a suspicion came to him. Suppose, just suppose, that while his mother was in the hospital at Iyienu recovering from what he could only deduce was overwork, this so-called father of his was having a good time with one of the girls? He tried to look closely into Pa's face but it was like a blank mask. Nevertheless the suspicion remained.

Clifford still thought of Ojebeta. He took it for granted that she would be his, when he was ready for her. He tried to make things easier for her, in the most subtle ways he could without arousing

119

speculation. However, what with his mother's illness, and his helping to run the stall and his determination to make a success of it, his hands were too full, his mind too occupied to think much of her.

The running of the stall was not an unqualified success, though at least it kept Ma's name at Otu. Clifford could not persuade his father to let Chiago go to the market every day, but on those days when she was allowed to go customers still patronised them.

It was on one of these market days that Chiago started to be ill. The Singer sewing-machine she used had been jingling and jangling as usual through the constant buzz of the market. Then suddenly Chiago stopped sewing and bent her head over the machine. Ijeoma was the first to notice, but she said nothing, thinking that something must be amusing Chiago and that she was trying to cover a laughing face. However Chiago did not lift her head up for a very long time. Even Clifford who was just then strolling into the stall saw her and immediately asked,

"You can't be going to sleep in the middle of the afternoon, are you, Chiago?"

Chiago lifted her head. Her eyes were very red as if she had been crying, though there were no tears at all visible. She opened her mouth to say something but her lips might as well have been glued together.

"Oh, no, don't tell me you've chosen this particular time to get a fever?" Clifford enquired, anxiety mixed with annoyance. "Do you think you can just hold on till you finish that lappa you are mending? Then we will all go home together in the evening, and Pa can give you one of his all-purpose medicines."

Clifford was being kind to ask whether she could hold on till evening, but had she any choice? She simply had to cling on. Chiago had by this time grown into a shapely beauty of twenty-two who would have been long married had she been living with her own people. But Ma and Pa Palagada, for reasons best known to themselves, had kept her as she was with them. She did a great deal of work, and the fact that Pa Palagada was very fond of her was becoming common knowledge. Chiago herself rarely talked about it. Not even now, when her mistress was away sick and Pa had come for her many times in the middle of the night to go to his room, did she complain at all. At first she had cried and rebelled against him in her heart, but to whom was she to complain? Who would listen to her? Pa could be quite tender and solicitous towards her when not drunk, but these kinds of nights left her tired and sleepy in the

mornings. Nonetheless she had never been ill like this before.
The familiar market buzz seemed like a hive of bees inside her
head. Her eyes felt as if they had decided to burst out of her head.
She told herself that unless she stopped sewing she would end up
sewing her fingers instead. Ijeoma watched her for a while, staring
at Clifford and opening and shutting her mouth, then attracted the
attention of Nwayinuzo who was attending a customer. Nwayinuzo
got the message and coughed — her particular method of soliciting
notice, well known to anyone accustomed to her ways. She wanted
to attract Clifford's attention but was too frightened to come
straight out with what she had to say. She knew that all was far
from well with her friend and room-mate Chiago.

"Master Clifford, I will take over Chiago's work if you will let
me. It is only that lappa that she has to finish and it's straight
sewing so it should not be difficult at all. She isn't well."

Clifford frowned and looked at the two girls. Nwayinuzo was
shaking nervously from her efforts to speak her mind for once to
the master; as her eyes darted this way and that she looked like an
animal about to run. On the other hand Chiago was drooping like
a dying flower. It seemed as if she no longer cared about anything he
might say but was keen to sink into a feverish sleep.

"Yes, take her work from her. And since Ijeoma is going home,
then to the hospital to look after Ma, Chiago should go with her."
He looked carefully at the older girl again, a puzzled look on his
face. "What is the matter with you?"

"I am ill in the belly and my head aches," Chiago mumbled
apologetically.

"All right, you go home with Ijeoma, and when you get home
look for Pa. He went to a market council meeting at Cable Point
in Asaba this morning; he should be back by now. Tell him what
the matter is with you and he will give you something to drink."

Clifford smiled to himself as he said this, for he knew that all
his father would ever give the slaves and servants was Epsom salt.
If you were a servant and you had a footache, you would have to go
to Pa and you would be given Epsom salt in warm water. Even if
it was your eyes which were sore, you would be treated likewise.
The taste of that Epsom salt was horrible. Everybody hated it, but
Pa derived malicious pleasure from seeing to it that his victims
swallowed the stuff in a few gulps, and very fast. He probably
thought that would deter them from pretending to be ill, particularly since the doses he gave had a way of purging everything in

121

one's inside except the internal organs, and it was likely that even those were bleached by the powerful brew.

Clifford was wrong. Pa was not yet home, so Ijeoma left Chiago with Ojebeta before taking the fresh fruit she had brought from the market on to Ma Palagada in hospital.

Pa had been delayed at the meeting — which had been called to discuss what action was to be taken about the unwelcome rules and regulations the white men were trying to introduce — when his fellow members began scolding him for being too friendly with the U.A.C. Europeans. He had to stay longer than he had anticipated, attempting to prove to his colleagues and fellow traders that if they were to carry out a massacre of the Europeans, what had befallen the Oba of Benin would happen to them. But he was not listened to. Instead Pa Palagada was called a coward, a lover of the white man. One member even went so far as to demand why he would not defend them, since was it not a fact that his so-called wife was a white man's cast-off? Had Pa ever been able to find an indigenous girl of his own?

This was so painful and so biting that Pa Palagada rushed at the man as if to murder him; luckily for both of them there were some of Pa's friends at the meeting, and they restrained him. "Can't you take any joke?" they said.

Nevertheless Pa Palagada knew the Ibo saying that you speak the truth when you are drunk, or when you say you joke. He became annoyed, took the earliest canoe that came along, crossed the river, with big Jienuaka his loyal slave, and walked home in long, angry strides. All the way he roared and thundered like a mad bull. He did not see any reason why they, the Ibo traders along the Niger, should not have man-to-man discussions with the Europeans. "If we kill them and they go, who will trade with us then? They will take all our possessions from us, so why can't we reason with them? Accusing my wife and me of going to their church and drinking tea in the afternoons! What has that to do with it anyway? It's jealousy. Just because we are getting on well, getting rich, they think it's because we go to the C.M.S. church. . . ." So ran Pa Palagada's thoughts on his way home. He knew too that he would have to tread carefully: if all the others turned against him and his wife things would be hard for them.

"I wish these stupid white men would not ask our women to pay tax," he thought, by way of compromise. "That will worsen the whole issue."

At home he bellowed at everyone until he was given his afternoon meal. Then he decided within himself that he and Ma Palagada would give moral support to whatever was decided by the market council, but that they would not take physical part in it. It was when he was in the midst of these thoughts, picking his teeth at the same time, that Ojebeta knocked to deliver the message about Chiago.

He heard the first knock and judged by the timidity of it that it was made by one of the girl slaves. But then he thought that they should all have gone to the market, and ignored the knock in his own particular way of instilling fear into the mind of whoever was there. The knock came again, a second and a third time.

"Who in hell is it?"

"It is only me," Ojebeta replied, moving a few steps away from the door as if she was expecting the tiger in the room to pounce on her, on sight.

"Come in, and what do you want, eh? Speak up, girl — what do you want?"

Ojebeta tried to still her beating heart, then heaved her lungs full of air and shouted, as though she was addressing a deaf giant. "Chiago is ill and she needs medicine!"

"What? What medicine. . . ."

"Chiago is ill—" Ojebeta began again, but was cut short by Pa Palagada, who was now standing, his voluminous house lappa open to reveal his overhanging stomach.

"I heard you. I am not deaf. Er . . . tell the girl Chiago to come here. Go and call her quickly. Don't stand there, go!"

When Ojebeta came to the room where they rested, she saw that Chiago was seemingly asleep, murmuring occasionally. She wished she did not have to wake her. She looked so tired and as if she needed some peace. All the same Ojebeta dared not anger their master.

"Wake up, Chiago, Pa wants to give you some medicine. Wake up. . . ."

Ojebeta took Chiago to the door of Pa's room but left her to go in by herself. She stood listening by the door — a bad habit for which they had all been punished many times — expecting Pa to roar at Chiago and ask her what gave her the audacity to be ill. But instead Ojebeta heard, unbelievingly:

"Now what's the matter with my little mother? Come — oh, how hot you are. . . ."

123

Ojebeta fled. That was how people talked to their wives. What did it mean? Inexplicably her mind went back to the conversation she had overheard between Chiago and Nwayinuzo, and also to what Clifford had told her only a few weeks before. Somewhere there was a connection. . . . She was confused, her head swam. She did not have much time to think further about it, for one of Victoria's little daughters was calling her urgently to come and help her with her akasi soup; she had spilt some on her clothes and now wanted Ojebeta to take it all away.

What with clearing up the soup and quieting the child, and changing them both for the evening, Ojebeta had little time to think about Chiago.

For days afterwards, though, she wondered what had happened. She remembered seeing the quarrelsome cook, Ma Basi, taking a bowl of hot soup into Pa's part of the house, though she could not be sure whom the soup might be for on such a hot afternoon. Neither could she tell why she had not been called to provide the lukewarm water that usually went with Epsom salt. The whole thing was even more mysterious to her since she no longer slept in the room with her friends or associated much with them in their part of the yard, and was too busy to have the time to go and discuss it with them. Besides, everyone seemed to assume that what was happening was the most natural thing in the world.

It was a very long time before Ojebeta saw Chiago again. And how many things had changed by then.

To everyone's joy and relief, Ma Palagada soon came back from the nursing home after being away in all for about twenty days. She was not as strong as she had been, neither was she as light-hearted; but she was back, and that called for a series of celebrations. Ma was back, weak but alive.

11 Women's Taxation

The fact that Ma Palagada had been to the jaws of death and back was talked about, among friends who felt glad for her, among enemies who regretted her not dying, and among the ordinary people who shrugged their shoulders and went on with their daily work. But in the Palagada household it was an occasion for joy.

Ma soon began to regain her lost energy. Her loud laugh could now be heard once more, and many of her friends started to visit the house again. Underneath all the gaiety and congratulatory messages, however, people who had known the family before sensed that things had changed and were changing even faster than the members of the household were able to realise. It surprised Ojebeta that no one commented on Chiago's absence.

Being a good Christian and given to good works, Ma had to have a thanksgiving service for her recovery. It was almost like another harvest festival. Ojebeta and the others took out their muslin dresses; by now they also had new accessories to complete their glamorous outfits. How excited Ojebeta, Amanna and Nwayinuzo were to be given proper cloth shoes with heels and laces. It turned out that it had been impossible to find a pair in Ijeoma's size, though she was later to have some silver earrings that dangled in her ears. On the eve of the thanksgiving day, Ma's daughter Victoria summoned Ojebeta into her bedroom.

"Come here, I want to talk to you."

Ojebeta did not at first know what to make of this invitation. She knew that Victoria could be brutal and really spiteful when she wanted to, but for some reason Ojebeta was no longer afraid of her at all. She felt that Victoria was seeking Ma's favour, and that she lacked the confidence which her sister Elizabeth and her brother Clifford had.

"I shall soon be going back to Bonny to be with my husband.

Would you like to come with us? The children like you so. They are used to you. My husband is a teacher so he will be able to help you, and then, when you are ready, you will marry over there, and have a house and children of your own."

Yes, and be forever reminded that I am a slave and have any child of mine called one, that is if I live long enough to have children, Ojebeta thought, as she gazed down at the raffia mat she had washed and polished that very morning. She did not dare lift her eyes to meet those of Miss Victoria, but she was not unaware of the fact that the latter was searching for hers, wanting to read in her expression what she was thinking. The fact that she was being asked showed that, for some reason or other, she could not be forced to go with her.

So she compromised and said, "Whatever Ma says, that I will do."

Victoria smiled — the first time Ojebeta had seen her smile — and nodded. "I knew you were a sensible girl and that you would say exactly that. Of course I will talk to *my* mother." she stressed the word "my" as if it was a threat to Ojebeta, as if she was warning her that her fate had already been decided.

Ojebeta felt a sense of panic and prayed inwardly: *Please, dear God, no, please, God, no — must I be a slave for ever?*

"Clifford went to Port Harcourt yesterday and bought two pairs of these. You wear one pair and the other will be for one of the other girls."

"Oh, thank you, Miss Victoria, thank you," she said, kneeling her gratitude as she put the shiny silver-plated earrings on. They were shaped like roses, with a large leaf dangling at the bottom of each. They were the very first earrings Ojebeta had ever had. She was so overjoyed that she forgot to wonder whether it might not be some kind of bribe.

When she was about to leave the room, Victoria's cool voice reminded her:

"Think about what I have just told you."

If this had been said as a calculated method of shaking her and draining her immediate happiness, it did just that. Had Ojebeta not been a slave, maybe what she would have done in that split second would have been to pull the silvery earrings from her ears and fling them at this arrogant person. But she could do nothing of the kind. She simply kept a strained smile on her face, nodded, and rushed out of the room.

126

What was the point of being unhappy about it? She would have had to wear them to show her appreciation of the gift whether she liked the earrings or not; but she did genuinely like them. Together with the shoes she had been bought on the previous market day — Ma had called them canvas shoes, and they had white wool markings on them and their edges were also trimmed with a kind of silky white — they gave her immense pleasure.

Later in the evening, when their house was being filled with people who had come for a taste of the food and drinks before the actual day of thanksgiving, and Ojebeta was busy handing drinks to this guest and sliced cassava to that one, Clifford touched her gently on the arm. She stopped and smiled at him shyly. She saw that he had been drinking, for the extra brightness in his eyes betrayed him.

He touched her ears. "I am glad you like them. I want you to wear them tomorrow, too, to the church." As soon as he had said this, he seemed to recollect himself, and quickly went over to one of his friends who had been watching him.

So he bought them for me, Ojebeta thought, *and that woman wanted me to think that it was her own idea — as if a woman like that would ever give anything to anybody.* She was even happier now that she had not flung the earrings in Miss Victoria's face.

The sun shone from early in the morning on the day of thanksgiving. Ma and Pa had paid for an orchestra known as the Kalabars, who had woken the whole neighbourhood. Relatives came from all over Onitsha, some representatives even came from Ma's people in Asaba. It was a huge crowd that danced with Ma in the streets to the new European music of the Kalabar drummers. The church filled to capacity. When Ma went to the front of the altar for special prayers to be said over her you could have heard a hairpin drop; then the sing-song voice of the vicar gave thanks to God for sparing the life of this very useful sister of the community. He called Ma a "pillar" of the Church, and all the congregation nodded.

Ojebeta opened her eyes and watched from where she sat at the back with her friends. She eased her hot feet out of the beautiful shoes. She watched Ma rise and put a fat envelope on the tray the vicar placed in front of her. Ojebeta marvelled silently at the heavy sound the envelope made as it dropped —

127

there must have been a lot of money in it! After that, all Ma's people went up, in their plush velvet and damask, to offer money to God for saving Ma from her illness.

The rest of the day was taken up with eating, drinking, eating again. Several cooks came from different households to assist Ma Basi, the Palagadas' cook. Even she managed for once to be in a good temper. Ma seemed happy too, though Ojebeta had a feeling that it was a forced happiness.

Ojebeta missed Chiago, for she had always been very helpful to Ma on occasions like today and was a quietly cheerful girl. Ojebeta wondered where she had gone. She prayed she would not have to go to Bonny with Victoria, so she might be able to have her old job back and sleep in the same room as her fellow slaves; then she could ask them what had happened to Chiago.

Ma was determined to go to her stalls on the very next market day. They were all busily stacking the new abada arrivals in the small room that served as the storeroom, when suddenly they could hear angry voices raised from the part of the house where Ma Palagada had her room. Ijeoma and Ojebeta stopped their work to listen. They did not have to strain their ears very much to hear Ma's enraged voice saying to someone:

"You could not even wait until I am dead and gone before you start sharing out my property! You all wanted me dead, I know that. See what happened to Chiago, the moment my back was turned."

"Mother, Mother — just listen. Don't get yourself worked up. You are still not very well. If you do not want her to go to Bonny with Victoria, then why should she go? She may be a very poor relation but, Mother, I like her. . . ."

As suddenly as the voices had flared up, so they faded to a whisper. Try as they might, the two girls could hear nothing distinctly, only murmurs. They looked at each other with worried frowns, decided that they could make out nothing from the little they had heard, shrugged their shoulders, and then continued putting one pile of material on top of another, in preparation for carrying it to the market.

Then they heard a door slam so loudly that they jumped. Miss Victoria in her slim elegance marched out of their part of the house and came to where the girls were attending to the bundles of cloth. She obviously wanted to say something to Ojebeta but, seeing Ijeoma there, decided against it and after a while said unnecessarily:

"Hurry up your packing. We must make some good sales today. I am going back to Bonny tomorrow, now that *my* mother is so much better."

"Yessima," the two girls chorused, wondering why this piece of information was being divulged to them. After all, they were only slaves, not full human beings.

Ojebeta suspected what might have happened, that maybe Ma Palagada was annoyed that Miss Victoria wanted her, Ojebeta, to go with her to Bonny to be her nursery slave. And maybe Clifford had told his mother that he wanted Ojebeta as a wife; his kitchen wife, at least, if not the elegant parlour one, for in those parts, Christian or no Christian, you were allowed as many wives as you could afford. In fact Ojebeta was correct in her suspicion.

"But, son, this is serious," Ma was saying to Clifford. "Why did you not tell me long ago? I would have spent more on her upbringing — and, look, I paid for her."

"Well, you can regard what you paid for her as her bride price. After all, you once told me that her brother had said you could give her away to whichever husband you wished when she grew up, and that you should regard her as your own daughter forever."

"Yes, there can be no doubt about that. I bought her body and soul. Still I feel we should have given her some more sophisticated training."

"Is it too late for that? Has she become a woman yet? We still have a few months or years to wait."

"Your father is not going to like it, but I personally feel very happy inside myself. I don't want you to marry one of these modern lazy, good-for-nothing women, who have grown up in luxury and want to be waited on hand and foot."

Clifford smiled, knowing Ma Palagada was referring to her own daughters who by now were used to lives of indolence.

Subsequently Ma did not waste much time in giving Ojebeta the special training that would prepare her for her new expectations. She did not think it wise to ask the girl's opinion; in fact she would have been shocked at the suggestion that Ojebeta might have other dreams. Clifford was her only son, and one day the big house would belong to him, as would all her money and the land she had bought in places like Asaba and Bonny. Her two daughters would take all her jewellery and clothes, but a girl who married her son Clifford was not marrying some petty trader with a shack for a stall, but an established one. She had put his name down for the new shops being built along the avenue, where he would be able to sell not only cloth but also durable things like sewing-machines and corrugated iron sheets for the new types of buildings that were then beginning to spring up all over Iboland at that time. No, her son was going to be a rich trader, and with a wife who had been brought up in the same trade life would be rich for both of them.

Ojebeta was by no means a bad-looking girl. Her greatest assets were her carriage — for she was straight as a palm, a feature she inherited from her parents — and her white teeth which flashed every time she smiled. She had very shiny black hair, which Ma made sure was cut very closely to her head every other week to avoid her having lice. Her skin was of the darkest brown possible without being actually black. Her face, too, would have been as smooth and beautiful as her body were it not for the leafy patterns her parents had had tattooed on her cheeks and forehead. One of her inner qualities was that Ojebeta did not know how to tell lies; in fact perhaps sometimes she was too outspoken to be tactful, just like the majority of people from Ibuza who prided themselves on being capable of speaking their mind, whatever the consequences. All in all, Ma Palagada was sure in her heart that she had been given her money's worth in Ojebeta.

Ojebeta was surprised when she was promoted to do the type of sewing which had been Chiago's job before she disappeared. On the next market day Ma, who had to take things easy, taught the girls the intricacies of taking detailed measurements and Ojebeta was allowed to make an attempt at sewing her first blouse. She was surprised yet again to learn, three market days later, that she was to keep the blouse for her very own use.

Miss Victoria left as she said she was going to, and a few days after that Ma sent her a girl they had brought from Aba, though money had not been paid for her outright since it had become illegal and more difficult to buy girls in such big places as Aba and Onitsha. Freed from the constant responsibility of attending Victoria's children, Ojebeta went back to her former room-mates, and was once more able to share confidences with her friend Amanna. Disappointingly, neither Amanna nor Ijeoma had any news about

Chiago, though they all had their suspicions. Nwayinuzo thought that perhaps she had been sold.

"They probably killed in the night, for some burial or something," said Amanna.

"Surely people don't do things like that these days," Ojebeta protested, her heart beating fast, "not in places like Onitsha."

"Even if they did do such a thing, who would tell them to stop? We have nobody to plead for us. Our people don't even know of our existence. I've thought and thought about it, but I can't find a solution."

"Ojebeta and I heard Ma saying something about Chiago, didn't we, Ojebeta? But she didn't mention any details."

Ojebeta nodded. After this they said nothing, for their thoughts went different ways.

Ojebeta knew for sure that she was being singled out for something better when she was enrolled in the "academy" which Mrs Simpson ran in her front parlour. There girls were taught how to bake cakes from maize flour, how to lift their long dresses decorously when they walked to church; they were taught how to crochet and how to embroider chain-stitches in patterns. Ojebeta was delighted and she asked no questions. If Clifford was to be her husband, and if Ma had agreed, then it was logical that they should want her to be educated in all this.

Her heart still bled for her own people, though. If only her mother had not died. If only her father had been spared to see his daughter now. But they were dead; there was no one to be proud of her little achievements. Sometimes the only consolation she could find was in the fact that had her father been alive, she probably would never have come to Otu in the first place and might not have known the kind of life she was now enjoying.

The truth of this latter aspect was always brought home to her whenever she went to the waterside after market was over to collect fresh fish for the evening meal. Then she would see her people, the people of Ibuza, in tattered clothes patched together in colours that did not match and in various stages of disintegration. Sometimes Ojebeta would venture to say "Welcome" to them, and they would invariably answer with beaming smiles. One or two of them wondered who she was, for her tribal face marks were not of the type normally to be found among Onitsha people. She had not encouraged them to talk to her, in case she was discovered by any of the Palagada household.

131

Ojebeta was one of the few Palagada girls lucky enough to be able to remember who her people were and to have been old enough to be able to recall the first love her parents had showered over her. Over the years such thoughts had magnified and grown right inside her head until that whole time before she was sold now seemed completely golden in her mind's eye. The other girls, on the other hand, could not even remember where they came from, nor did Ma divulge where they had originally been bought. They all knew vague stories of their origins but could not point out exactly where their villages were. Ojebeta could and she talked about it many a time, much to the annoyance of the others, so if any of them had caught her talking to the people from Ibuza at the waterside there might be trouble for her.

One evening Ma Palagada came back to her stalls from one of the innumerable market meetings, very flustered and sad. Ojebeta was sitting on a stool opposite her with heaps of lappas she was finishing, while Ma from her velvet-covered seat began to talk to no one in particular.

"I am not going to take part in such senseless fighting. Why can't the men do it themselves? Why can't we talk things over with the white men? It is all silly and idiotic. . . ."

As if Ma's voice had been carried by the wind to Ma Mee's stall, the latter walked up to Palagada in all her majesty and spoke in a voice that was not too friendly.

"Why do you not wish to fight the so-called white men? Because you are their friend? Don't you know that if we women have to pay tax it will affect you also? You too will have to pay tax. Did you ever hear of a country where women are asked to pay for their existence? No, we must nip it in the bud."

The woman in the stall opposite Ma Palagada's, Madam Okeke — one of the very few Onitsha traders who was thin — came over as well, visibly agitated and angry at Ma Palagada.

"We look towards people like you and your husband, Palagada, to help us," she said shrilly, "and now you're being lukewarm about it."

Ma Palagada could take all these accusations no more. She stood up, drawing herself up to her full height and bulk, and thundered at the two women at the small crowd that was beginning to gather in front of her stall.

"If you feel that I'm a Judas, you are lying. Go on and kill the missionaries and white traders, go on! I don't say that we should

132

pay taxes. What my husband and I are saying is that we should all refuse to pay, and let them do their worst."

"But they are your friends, these so-called missionaries. Pooh! The so-called people of God!" sneered Madam Okeke as she chewed something furiously in her mouth. She was a very bitter woman, who always tied her lappa tightly round her waist as if she was ready to go to war at any time of the day. One could see the nerves in her forehead twitching as she attacked Ma verbally. Her angry eyes wandered and took in everything in Ma Palagada's stall, saying eloquently with that action: *How else could you have managed to gather so much wealth if not for the reason that you warm yourself to the white people in our midst?*

Without looking at Madam Okeke, Ma Palagada sensed what was going on in her mind and what all these people were thinking. Trade was not as profitable as it used to be during the days of the legitimate slave traders. Now the Niger people had to rely on trading in palm kernels and cloth, mainly cotton from Lancashire in England; and these new types of trade required a great deal of capital investment, rather than just physical strength. If only these people could think back far enough they would realise that Ma had started with very good resources and that her present wealth was not to be accounted for by the mere fact that she went on some evenings to the Simpsons' house to drink tea. And if they had bothered to check they would also have realised that Pa Palagada, although he might still take walks with his wife in the evenings as the Church encouraged husbands to do, was not all that faithful or in love with her. But people's memories could be so short, and their eyes could be so blind when they refused to see.

She remembered a saying of the people of Ibuza, where her mother had come from, that if you cooked dinner for the crowd, the crowd would finish it and even ask for more, but if the crowd should decide to cook dinner for you, an individual, you could never finish it. She had to compromise, to save herself, her family, and to preserve her health, which was still playing her up.

"All right," she said, stepping down and quickly agreeing with them, "when you are ready, I shall be ready too. I'm not paying any tax, that much I know. Maybe when they see how determined we are, they will let our custom be — the custom that says only our men should pay for their heads, because they own us."

"E-hem, that's good talk. If we don't stop them now, they will soon be telling us to pay for the unborn babies in our bellies," Ma

133

Mee said by way of conclusion. Then she took a closer look at Ma Palagada and said in a low silky voice tinged with pity: "You are not fully recovered, my friend. Take good care of yourself. A lot depends on you, you know."

Ma Palagada smiled sadly. "If I drive the sandfly away from my body, whom do I want it to bite? My daughters? My son? No, it is better it bites me."

The other women went back to their stalls, thoughtful that Ma Palagada who was so well known as a great fighter should give in so easily. Many assumed that she had done so to safeguard her property and her trade, for few Onitsha traders would underestimate the power of an irate crowd.

That was all that the girls knew of it, though most of the days which followed were full of suppressed activity. Ma and Pa started to argue openly, and Ma would invariably lose her temper. All the work of looking after Ma and coming into close contact with her was now gradually falling to Ojebeta. Many an evening Ma preferred to have her meal in her bedroom, and Ojebeta would have to wait on her.

On one such occasion, Ma said to her all of a sudden: "You have grown, Ojebeta, and this house has suited you. Your father would be glad."

"Thank you, Madam," Ojebeta replied, curtsying as she had now been taught by Mrs Simpson.

"I would like you to go and visit your people some day, after you have fully settled with Clifford. They will be so surprised to see you. And, Ojebeta, I want you to remember that we get something as sweet as honey from bees that sting. So try and forgive your brother. Now you are going to be my son's wife, take care of him. All that would never have come about if your brother Okolie had not sold you to me. But in this household you will cease to be a slave the day you and my son Clifford marry."

"Yes, Madam." This was followed by another curtsy. What was there for her to say? She counted herself lucky, and it would have sounded ungrateful if she had expressed her wishes otherwise. Thank God that they would let her see her people; that was something she could look forward to.

On her way from Ma Palagada's room she almost collided with Clifford. She greeted him with the Ibo welcome, "Nnua," and walked away quickly.

He stood watching her for a long time, noting the differences in her behaviour.

"Ojebeta is now quite a little miss," he commented to his mother. "I think it suits her."

"She is a nice girl, very humble. And she is a cousin of yours, but none of her people would object anyway, for they have not seen her for years. Have you started talking to her, getting to know her?"

Clifford shook his head in the negative.

"Then you must start soon, whenever you see her sitting by herself. It boosts a woman's ego to think her consent is really sought in deciding her future."

"I know that, Mother, but when is she ever free? She is always working and working. . . ."

"Work is good for her; all the same, we shall need more servants to run this house. When I get really better, I shall have to go to Aba to see if I can find some good girls."

"It's impossible to find baby girls being thrown away among the Efiks any more," Clifford noted. "One missionary — Mary Slessor they call her — has saved many of them herself. And a lot of women are now getting to know that twins do not necessarily bring bad luck to a family."

"I don't even want a very young child. I am too old now to bring them up myself. I want a girl who is at least ten years old, and able to work. A servant, not a slave."

"You are well now, aren't you, Mother?" Clifford asked with sudden concern.

"Yes, I am all right. Why do you ask?"

"Nothing — only that you look tired. You should not go with them to the protest demonstration you helped the other women organise."

"I see what you mean. No, I cannot go, not only because I see no point in carrying cutlasses and clubs but because my head aches whenever there is so much noise."

On the day of the Aba riot, when the market women rebelled against being taxed, Ma Palagada was in her room, very ill; this time there was very little hope of her coming out of it alive.

12 Mushroom of Freedom

Ma Palagada's second illness was swift. It wasted no time in doing its worst. Her headaches became so blinding that she would cry for hours in agony, and later nature would relieve her of her pain by making her lapse into a kind of coma. She only missed one more market day. On the following Saturday, Ojebeta was in Ma's room, tidying things and wanting to know if Ma needed anything.

"Ogbanje Ojebeta!" Ma called her gently.

Ojebeta was startled, for no one had used her full name for a long while.

"You must stay by my son. Men are not as clever as they look. They always need someone, a woman to cook for them. Look after him for me."

"Yes, Madam. But you will be here with us. I mean, you will stay with us, when I am grown enough to be a woman."

"I am going on a long journey. . . ."

Then unexpectedly Clifford came in. He looked concerned, but his expression brightened a little when he saw Ojebeta very near his mother's bed.

"I was just telling your girl-wife that you should look after each other well."

"Mother, don't talk so, I don't like it. You are scaring Ojebeta. We shall take over the market after this horrid riot, and you will rest and not have to rush about so much. You will help us with our children. So don't talk like that."

Involuntarily, Clifford moved closer and touched Ojebeta. He put his arm round her waist, and fear and excitement ran through her. She could not give meaning to her feelings, though something was telling her that Ma would not be with them for much longer. Ojebeta slipped away from Clifford's hold and covered her face and cried — it was an indulgence which a normally arduous life of

136

servitude left her little time for and which the caning, humiliation and dehumanisation she had tasted in this household had taught her never to allow herself. Even Ma Palagada's characteristic benevolence had never been able to counteract the effects of the severe treatment meted out by her husband and her daughter. But now, for the first time in about nine years, Ojebeta felt that she was being regarded as a human being, and she found herself beginning to behave like one, rather than like a hardened slave who would feel no emotion at seeing her mistres die.

"It will be all right," she heard Clifford saying in her ear. "She hasn't fully recovered from the other illness, that is what's wrong. She will be better soon, you'll see. Won't you, Mother?"

"Yes. I will. . . ."

Then there were noises of welcome outside heralding the fact that Ma's daughter had descended on the house once again; and amid the noises of welcome the church bells were ringing, and ringing.

"What is happening in the church?" Ma asked.

"I don't know. Maybe it is for special prayers for you, and for this riot that our people are taking part in. Though the Mission wouldn't know about the riot — they have nothing to do with it. . . ." Clifford ended in a low voice, as if debating with himself.

"I'm going to church tomorrow. I must be there to pray to God to change people's hearts. Ojebeta, you must get my white velvet Christmas gown ready for me. Go, girl, and be quick, to catch the remaining sun. . . ."

Ojebeta went blindly from the room, to fetch the dress as she had been told.

Ma Palagada did go to the church that Sunday, as she had said she would, but she did not walk there: she was carried there in a coffin draped with countless tropical flowers. Young pride-of-Barbados with their fragile leaves were deftly twisted together against the crimson of lake lilies with their exotic leaves. Myriads of hibiscus flowers were sewn or stuck to the sweet-smelling leaves of lantana plants.

For the time being, Ma's death seemed to make people forget their earthly troubles and stop to think that, after all, we were all here on earth for just a short while.

For the innocent girls she had brought from their various places

137

of birth and given shelter and home for all these years, their sorrows were too much to bear. The question "What is to be our fate now?" loomed for them all, defined in the vacant expressions on their faces. Ijeoma wept silent tears as the hundreds of mourners who turned up to bid Ma a final farewell ordered her to do this, fetch that, wash something else. Nwayinuzo too was worked so hard that she felt almost dizzy.

By night time, when there were very few hours of darkness left, the girls were too stunned and too afraid to begin having any kind of plans or deliberation straight away. It was little Amanna who said wistfully,

"I wish I had a father who would now come and claim me, now that our kind Ma is gone."

"So do we all," Nwayinuzo said in the darkness. "Now it all depends on Pa, and what he thinks of us. O God . . . help us," she choked into her night lappa.

"Ojebeta, you are going to be all right, aren't you? Aren't you going to Miss Victoria's house or something?" Ijeoma wanted to know.

"I wish I could say for certain what is going to happen. I can't tell you yet because I'm not sure myself."

"Ma always had good plans for you, because her parents also came from Ibuza, didn't they? At least you know who your people are."

"Yes, I know I do. But how many times have you seen any of my people coming here to ask of me? Suppose I have to go there, and then find that I'm not wanted — what will happen to me then? Should I come back here to the only home I have known for all these years?"

"Hmmm," sighed Nwayinuzo, "it is sad. This place is not the same without Ma Palagada. It is the end of the story. What we will have from tomorrow will be the beginning of another story. We may be part of it or we may be plucked out like foot lice. Let's go to sleep, and at least get our energy back for the new order."

Amanna could be heard crying. Lucky girl; at least she was able to relieve the heavy pain in her young heart by giving vent to tears. The others could not.

The new order that Nwayinuzo had foretold did indeed begin the very next day. Mourners still poured in from all over Otu and the small towns and villages nearby. Miss Victoria's people had come from Bonny, Ma's other daughter Elizabeth who was married to a wealthy Yoruba lawyer came with her husband, a fat man with a very large belly and curious tribal marks cut on his face. He always wore traditional robes, and ate a great deal. The house was packed full for days and days.

The greatest surprise of all came around mid-morning, when the cooking and eating and hymn singing was still going on. Ojebeta went to attend to Pa, who was calling her furiously, and when she walked into his room whom did she see but Chiago, rocking on her knee a little baby boy. Ojebeta was stunned. She stood there by the door, just as if she had been turned into a piece of stone. Chiago saw her amazement and smiled.

"Ojebeta, are you well? How are the others? I will be coming to greet you all. I've just arrived and my child wanted some water. Come in."

"Welcome," stammered Ojebeta, wanting to run, for she saw that Pa Palagada was fixing her with a menacing look. "Welcome."

"Get the child a drink of water, and hurry up. Then come back and help them unpack."

In no time at all, it was clear to everyone that Chiago was going to be the new mistress. However, for a few days after Ma's burial Pa Palagada made it look as though Chiago had simply come back to help in the household; and indeed that was how things seemed. It was all done so cleverly that many people still regarded and treated her as a slave who had had the misfortune to have a baby. But people did ask, "Whose baby is he?"

Those concerned in the little drama were not saying anything. Pa Palagada was quite unapproachable. Even though Ma Palagada's daughters made many claims to her property, it was made clear to them that, although they were welcome to some of Ma's trinkets and some of the servants, her lands and her business were the concern of the males in her life.

"Have you ever seen such greedy daughters? They are not mourning for their dead mother; all they want are her goods." This was what Pa had made people believe.

Chiago helped to keep the household running, knowing from experience where everything and everyone was. So much so that on the last night before Ma's daughters left, when they wanted to go through Ma's trinkets, her gold and her velvets, they could find very little of any value. Victoria accused Pa of robbing them of their rights and he denied any knowledge of the loss of their mother's belongings. Elizabeth, whose husband was a lawyer, threatened to take the case to court. The noise and arguments that ensued were so disquieting and disgraceful that for once the servants felt really like running away.

Ojebeta too started to think seriously of running away. If this was going to be the pattern of their lives then she would rather go and leave these greedy people. She felt somewhat confused and hurt by Clifford's frequent absence from the house since Ma's death — was it that he was avoiding her, no longer found it convenient to humour her, or was it simply that he was kept busy seeing to business affairs connected with the market?

She was sitting on the back pavement with the others when her thoughts were cut short by Miss Victoria coming rapidly towards her.

"Ojebeta, Ojebeta! Where is that stupid girl? Ojebeta, come here. You must get ready. We are leaving for Bonny by the first ferry tomorrow morning. I want to leave this house as soon as possible. Do you hear me?"

"Yes, Madam." In one movement Ojebeta got to her feet and curtsied politely.

Miss Victoria hesitated for a moment, wondering who it was that had been teaching the girls all these nice manners. If she had not been in such a rage she would have enquired about it. As it was she said nothing. That girl must come with her. She was a hard worker and could help Victoria set up a business like her mother's. She strode away, and the other girls immediately started to talk.

"Oh, Ojebeta, so this is our last night together. Please don't cry. The good Lord who has helped you here will also help you in her house. Her children are very beautiful...."

They were trying to make things easier for her, and she knew it. But in fact all that was happening was that their sympathy was going in one ear and coming out the other. Where was Clifford in all these hasty decisions, she kept asking herself?

She remembered what Ma Palagada had said to her only the day before she died: that most men could not look after themselves, to say nothing of looking after those in their care. Should she or should she not seek him out and ask him what his decision was? Victoria obviously did not know what Ma's plans had been for Ojebeta. But if Clifford cared would he not have looked for her? Even if she had been bought — or paid for, or however they interpreted the transaction that had taken place between her brother and Ma Palagada in Otu market on that day long ago — she still had human feelings. No, she would rather go to her own people,

140

whatever doubts she may once have had. She would promise this family that if she ever married or ever belonged to somebody else, that person would refund to the Palagadas whatever Ma had given Okolie for her. She would tell her owners that in the morning; she would take her few small possessions and leave the house for good, after wishing them all goodbye.

Having thus made up her mind, Ojebeta went straight to the white basket with the cover which Ma had bought her, as well as one for each of the others. She remembered their great joy on the day Ma had bought the baskets, how thrilled she in particular had been to own her very special clothes container. Since then Ojebeta had acquired a few bits and pieces — the first blouse she had made, her very own table cloth with the picture of a fish she had sewn there in plain stitch, her two lappas and blouses, and of course her most prized possessions, her real silver-plated earrings and the matching chain Ma had recently given her. Then there was another dress of hers, a cotton one with green leaves worked on it, with its neck and puffed sleeves piped in white: this was the dress that she promised herself she would wear on her first Sunday back in Ibuza. Then she saw her charm bells.

She could not remember for certain whether her home village had a church or not. There were now so many churches all over Otu and church-going had become so much part of her life that she could not envisage any village, however remote, where there would not be a place of worship. In fact what gave her the most heartache about the thought of leaving Otu Onitsha was that she had just started to attend baptism classes; she hoped she would have the opportunity to continue them when she went home to Ibuza.

Ojebeta slept peacefully after that, to the great surprise of all her comrades in suffering.

In the morning she went as usual with the others to the river to wash and fetch water for the cooking. The other girls saw her mood and did not ask questions for they themselves were wondering what was going to happen to them. When they returned to the house, Ojebeta called Amanna softly.

"Do you still have my share of the money we got when we did that dance during the harvest?" she asked.

"Yes, I buried it, where we buried the canes." It had been their habit to hide those of the canes which they found most bitingly painful. Pa never missed any of them, for whenever he went to the villages in the river delta he was bound to come home with a brand

141

new cane in tow. The girls, knowing how difficult it was to burn young green bamboo, usually buried them instead.

"Do you want your share, then?" Amanna asked, her voice low and tremulous.

Ojebeta nodded. After a pause she added, "I want to go back to my people."

Amanna looked away as if to try to hide her face. She would miss Ojebeta, but if she could go back to her people, that would be the best thing for her. She told her so.

"If your people really don't want you, you can come back, and maybe you would be allowed to work here for pay until you earn enough to give back all the money your brother took from Ma. For you know the curse that every slave bought is under, that you are never really free until you have repaid what was paid for you or until the actual person who bought you sets you free."

"I know. That's why I am not secretly running away. I shall tell them all that in the big house, and promise to pay them back one day. My bride price will be enough to do that, because my brother told Ma to free me as soon as my future husband repaid her with my bride price."

Amanna opened her eyes wide, and covered her mouth in astonishment. "You want to tell them you are leaving? They won't let you!"

"You remember that parable Jesu said, that a house divided against itself shall not stand? Well, this house is divided against itself. Ma never wanted me to go away with Victoria; but Victoria wants somebody she can own body and soul, an everlasting servant. Pa would do anything to hurt Victoria, because she isn't his daughter. And Clifford doesn't seem to be as—" she paused, searching for a suitable word — "reliable as Ma was. So I think this is the right time for me to move, before someone else inherits me."

"I think you're very wise. God will help you, I know it," said Amanna conclusively, as she sneaked out of the room on her way to the lantana bush in the back yard to fetch Ojebeta's share of their dance money, which had been buried for months. It was not just the dance money, but whatever little amounts had come their way they had kept together in this common fund. Often after a heavy breakfast they had saved their lunch money, not necessarily because they were too full but because agidi Accra, though a delicacy to those who came to the market only once in a while, could become boring when taken frequently. So they buried their money,

142

to save it being discovered, and because they knew that if they did it that way nobody would tell on anyone else.

Amanna was pleased to note that Ojebeta's share was a whole ten English shillings and two and a half pennies. She wondered what would be done with Chiago's share, since she had left without telling any of them and was now a very prestigious servant with a child of her own. Amanna hoped she would be able to talk to the others before Ojebeta left.

"Hey, you there! Ojebeta!" Miss Victoria was soon standing in the back veranda and shouting. "Hurry up, we have to catch an early ferry. Ojebeta! Ojebeta! God, where is that girl?"

Ojebeta emerged from the kitchen where she had been talking to Chiago, who for her part gave her blessing to her going away. Chiago had said to her that Ma had built too big an empire for those she left behind to be able to look after it properly. The other market women were jealous of her success, saying she was too friendly with the white people; her son Clifford was not accomplished in academic work; and her daughters were greedy, spoilt women. If Ojebeta had noticed that Chiago said nothing critical about Pa, she did not wish to remark upon it. Now that it actually came to telling Miss Victoria she was not going to Bonny with her, Ojebeta's heart was beating fearfully.

When Miss Victoria saw her coming without her basket, she yelled, "Get your clothes basket, girl! Did my mother not buy you one? Come on, go and get it. Don't waste my time!"

So arrogant was her voice and so commanding that Ojebeta, like someone in a trance, went to their room to fetch her basket. Amanna was not there, for the girls had dispersed to their various morning tasks. Picking up the basket and balancing it on her head, Ojebeta marched across the compound to the big house. But she did not go to Miss Victoria's room. She went to Pa Palagada's part of the house, and was not at all surprised to see Chiago there, with her baby on one side of her, picking up Pa's dirty clothes with her other free hand.

Ojebeta breathed in deeply, then spoke. "Pa Palagada, I want to go back to my people, now that Ma has gone. I thank you both for looking after me so well up till now. I don't want to go to Bonny with Miss Victoria — I can't even speak the Bonny language. . . ." Her voice started to falter and she was near to tears.

Pa studied her for a long time. Ojebeta had expected him to thunder as he was wont to do when Ma was alive, but his personality seemed to have changed. He was calmer now, more humane; he seemed like a contented person who did not wish to have his peace disturbed. He had been doing some kind of accounts but had stopped, and now he asked:

"Are you sure there will be people in your town who will look after you?"

Ojebeta held her breath to prevent herself from fainting. She had not expected this kind of response. Chiago gave her a conspiratorial look, as if to urge her on. It was a precious moment.

She nodded vigorously. Yes, her people would look after her.

"Then there is nothing to be said. If you marry one of your people, make sure they return Ma's money to her son Clifford, because I think she wanted you for him. However, I don't think Clifford knows what he wants."

"Sir, may I say something? Well, Ojebeta will not be living in the heavens — if Clifford wants to marry her, he can go to her people and make the arrangement. Her place is only Ibuza, where he can go and return in one day. Or, Ojebeta, would you like to wait for him to come back? He went to Aba, to see to Ma's interest in the riot that is taking place there."

"No, Chiago, I will go today. If Master Clifford wants to know where I am, he can come to Ibuza." She knew she had to hurry, before Miss Victoria resorted to bringing force to bear on her.

"You will need some money to pay for your ferry and to buy food and presents for your people. Take this," said Pa, proffering two of the pieces of coin known in those days as dollars. So Ojebeta was given the considerable amount of four shillings.

She thanked Pa, and quickly left the room, carrying her basket to the back yard to say a final farewell to her friends. But she walked into Miss Victoria, who this time was really irate.

"How dare you keep me waiting? Don't you know we'll miss the ferry?" She raised her right hand to strike as usual but Ojebeta used her clothes basket as a shield.

"I am not going to Bonny with you," she shouted defiantly. "I am going to my people. I'm going home!" Her heart was beating fast. Her eyes were round and shone with the first joy of freedom. "I'm going home."

"You can't go. We bought you. You'll be treated as a runaway slave. I will see to that. You must come with me."

"No, Miss Victoria, I will not come with you. I shall pay back every penny my brother borrowed from our mother who has gone,

144

and I shall pay it back to Clifford. She wanted me for Clifford, not for you. And Clifford is not here, so why should I go with you?"

"Then why should you go to your people, since Clifford is not in?" Miss Victoria retorted, cornering her.

"I'm going there to wait for him. When he wants me, he will come for me."

Victoria burst out laughing. "I must say that you slave girls certainly do have ambition. Chiago wanting to take over the whole household, and you wanting my brother to marry you? So that's the situation. Well, let me tell you, slave girl from Ibuza, this can never be so. You are a slave. Come with me, and you shall have your freedom in a few years, without having to repay a farthing."

Ojebeta recoiled from her; but she did not have the courage to answer back a superior. She was still considering how she could make a bolt for it and run when unexpectedly Miss Victoria snatched the clothes basket from her.

"Give me back everything my mother gave you, you ungrateful slave!"

Ojebeta saw her burrow her determined fingers into the clothes she had lovingly folded only the night before. She threw this garment one way, trampled on that one, so great was her anger. She fumed and cursed; and Ojebeta stood by in the corridor watching this madness. If she had been in any doubt about never returning to this household, there was none in her now. How could a kind person like Ma Palagada have given birth to such a vicious woman as this?

It soon became apparent that what Victoria was searching for were the trinkets Ma had given Ojebeta. She took the earrings, the silver bangles and the chain. She left all Ojebeta's cherished clothes scattered and trodden on. Then she flung back at her as she marched to her room:

"If you want these silver trinkets back, you will have to come to Bonny to get them!"

Ojebeta knew that the pieces of jewellery were precious and that Ma had given them to her confident in the knowledge that she might one day marry her son Clifford. If Ma had wanted her to remain a slave in perpetuity, she would not have given them to her. Now her selfish daughter, in a fit of pique and disappointment at not inheriting from her mother all she had hoped for, was taking them away as a kind of revenge. Ojebeta was sorry about it, and really wanted those things, but she would rather be free than let herself be bought a second time.

With hot tears of sadness burning her eyes, she bundled the clothes back into the basket, quickly enough to avoid Chiago who was just coming out of Pa's room. She did not want to talk to anyone about this last humiliation. She could no longer bring herself to say goodbye properly to her friends in the yard, and in her confused state was forgetting the money she was to collect from Amanna. The latter realised what Ojebeta was about to do, and eagerly ran and caught up with her.

"Ojebeta, you're not leaving without saying goodbye to your unfortunate friends, are you? We heard what Miss Victoria said, and your decision. And I think you are very wise. Go to your people. Even if they can only afford to give you mushroom instead of meat, you'll know that it is mushroom of freedom. This is your share of the money we all saved together, and Chiago said just now that we can share out hers as well. I think she is going to live in this house for ever. I wouldn't mind that at all."

"Thank you all very much, and extend my thanks to the men — Jienuaka and the others. I don't really know why I'm crying; but, believe me, I would rather be a poor girl in Ibuza than a well-fed slave in this house without Ma. So I should be really happy. I hope I can find something to do." She wiped the tears from her eyes.

"Oh, you will find plenty to do. Your people bring gallons of palm oil to Otu to sell. With the little money you have you won't have to press the oil yourself, you can just buy it from the home pressers and come here to sell it. So the work won't be so bad as to make you haggard, like those poor Ibuza people we see at Asaba and Otu carrying akpu and oil."

"I will remember that. And please thank Chiago for me. Whenever I come to Otu, I shall always look for you."

Ojebeta glanced back only once at the building that had been her home for the past nine years. She did not regret anything, though the death of Ma still hurt her as if she had been her real mother. The house stood there in all its majesty, with its red shutters and its side gate. The tops of many guava trees and of the pawpaw ones at the back of the house were visible from the front. With a heavy heart she repeated to herself what she had been told by Amanna — that unfortunate young woman whose parents had thrown her away because she was one of a set of twins, that poor creature who did not know from which part of Calabar province she came.

Go to your people, and eat the mushroom of freedom if they cannot afford to buy you meat.

146

Yes, she would rather go back to Ibuza and eat the mushrooms that grew wild than stay in this house, and eat meat in slavery.

13 Home, Sweet Home

The people of Ibuza, living off the land, were poor. But when it came to claiming lost relatives few nations of the earth could be more generous with their welcome than Ibuza people.

The fact that Ojebeta had left home when she was only seven did not dim the warmth she knew she would receive from her people. She was right. After crossing to the other side of the river, she asked for the Ibuza stalls; these were not hard to find, for they sold mainly akpu, a pulp made from cassava, and palm oil. The markings on her face did the rest. Right there in the market she acquired tens of relatives. Women from her very own homestead in Umuisagba came and hugged her. The everyday clothes she was wearing were like velvet compared with the rags and faded outfits these women wore to market. Another great difference was in the way they talked which seemed brusque and loud to Ojebeta now. Also their skin, even that of young girls, seemed burnt, dark and rough, or dry and lacking in moisture. However, their open hearts compensated for these small defects.

They bought and gave her all kinds of food, and even though she assured them several times that she did not want any she was pressed to eat some yam, roasted and soaked in its skin and then soaked in palm oil till it dripped. But at least for the sake of the old woman who had bought it for her Ojebeta soon learned to like it. The woman had introduced herself as the senior wife of Ukabegwu; she was very wrinkled, with tobacco-dark teeth and a neck in which so many nerves and sinews stood out in relief. She reminded Ojebeta of what she had used to do for her when she was little, and, with a rather unpleasantly harsh laugh, told her many things about her mother Umeadi.

"She would have been glad to see her daughter back from *olu oyibo*, from working with the white people. You would have been

148

her pride and joy, with such smooth skin and such modest and polished manners. Oh, your aunt will be insane with happiness. Oh, they will be glad to know that felenza did its worst but did not kill off all our people. . . ." On and on she went. Then she joked, "Ogbanje Ojebeta, where did you leave your *ogbanje* charms?"

"I have them with me. They guided me. They reminded me of home."

And the senior wife of Ukabegwu said, in great joy: "You have outgrown those your friends from the other world. They will never worry you any more. But you should keep your charms. Your father faced death to get them for you."

They would not call Ojebeta's stay with Ma Palagada anything other than a good thing. For had she not returned with such fine manners and clothes, just like the older men who went to seek their fortune in the white man's jobs, in *olu oyibo*. No, it was to *olu oyibo* that she too had gone, not just to Otu Onitsha. That was an understatement.

In Ibuza, though there were at the time nothing like newspapers or bush radio, people had ways of spreading rumours fast. So it was no surprise to the little group that made their way from Asaba to see five young men and four women on their way to meet them. They all met in front of a big hut which was a mission station, newly built by some people who called themselves the Church Missionary Society and who talked about a new God called Jesu Christi.

Uteh, the senior daughter of Obi Okwuekwu, let go her tongue. She sang the praises of all their ancestors right down to Ogbanje Ojebeta, the daughter of Okwuekwu Oda. She had a piece of *nzu* — sacrificial chalk — in her hand, and she sprinkled some on each homestead god or goddess as they passed; she also left them pieces of kolanut. When they came to Umuodafe, a village at the extreme edge of Ibuza, she said to their god:

"Afo, have this chalk, and eat this piece of kolanut, for my daughter who I thought had died is back. Afo, eat kolanut. . . ."

She went on thus until they reached Ojebeta's people. It was then that Ojebeta found out that she had really not forgotten the lay of her homeland. She could see the market now, though it was smaller than it had been in her imagination. She saw other huts where she remembered her father's used to be, and knew that other relatives had taken the position. To her people land was a communal holding. You came during your lifetime and built your own hut, and when you died your hut was pulled down and burned and all your wealth

149

buried with you. So the land would be cleared ready for another generation. In Ibuza, people came and people went, but the communal land remained. It was a foolish person, therefore, who did not take care of his father's ancestral holding, for it was to there he would eventually return. Nobody owned land, for how could anyone own land, when you could not even own the air you breathed and the water you drank?

It was then that she asked, "Okolie, my brother — where is he?"

"Okolie has gone to *olu oyibo*, a long time ago, and so has your brother Owezim before him. They are in a place called Lagos. Your elder brother works in a big ship — as big as a village — and now he has four sons and a girl. Okolie . . . Okolie — we don't know much about Okolie. . . . But," added Uteh more brightly, "Okolie is still living. Life is more important than anything."

"I cannot stay here in Umuisagba, then, since Okolie is away, and my eldest brother has gone to a white man's job."

"Come and live with us. Don't you know that the great-grandfather of your father and my great-grandfather were of the same mother and father?" said old Ukabegwu, whose wrinkled wife had announced the arrival of their new relative. "So how can you think you have no father, when I am here? I hold your family *ofo*, the symbol of worship for your family; if your brother Owezim should die, your bride price will come to me."

"Nothing of the sort is happening," said Uteh. "I know that I am a woman and a daughter in this town, but I am the only living daughter of Obi Okwuekwu. Ojebeta's father and I had the same mother and father."

"But you are a woman!" shouted Ukabegwu's senior wife. "How is it that you want to inherit the girl? It is not your right!" In Ibuza women were usually more conservative than men.

Uteh knew that if she pursued the argument with force, she would lose Ojebeta for the second time. So she lowered her voice.

"I don't want her bride price. I only want her to come and rest with me for a while. But if during that time you were to need her to help you with something you wished to do, of course she would come here and help. For who is her father if not Ukabegwu?"

"Our people say that argument is like an old rag: if you dump it here it stays here, and if you dump it there it stays there. That is good talk, Uteh the daughter of Obi Okwuekwu. Let the girl stay with you. If there is anything that her duty calls her to come and help us out with, then she should come quickly.'"

This minor argument which had its origins in good faith might have marred Ojebeta's arrival; but it was tactfully quenched, and the dispute in Ukabegwu's senior wife's mind was suppressed, though not completely successfully. For there was a saying in Ibuza, that those who have people are wealthier than those with money; a young girl of sixteen, in her prime, attractive and strong, would have been a boon to a family such as the Ukabegwus. She could help to fetch water from the stream which was about three miles from the village, she could clay the house, fetch the family akpu, and she could even do some trading before she was married away to a husband. And when she married the chief woman who had looked after her would have a little share of a pound for her troubles. Food was not all that plentiful, but if one could work hard one would not starve in the dry season. As for the harvest season, there were more yams thrown away then and plantains given to the goats than people could possibly consume. The trouble was that people had no means of keeping the perishable food so that it would last them through the whole year.

Eze, Uteh's husband, was thrilled with their luck. Apart from the work she could do, they actually loved Ojebeta, and she was to spend the most enjoyable part of her adolescence with them. There were so many things she had to re-learn.

On the very next day after her arrival, her aunt was glad to see that she had already been to the stream and returned, just as she used to do at the Palagada house in Otu. Uteh called to her fondly.

"Ma'am," Ojebeta responded from the other side of their hut.

"What is this?" Uteh exclaimed in shocked tones. "We may not have been to *olu oyibo*, but here we are still people, not goats. Why is it that you answer like that when I call you? What does it mean? And when my husband called you last night you told him, 'Sah!' as if you were driving away a snake. What do you mean by it?"

Ojebeta patiently explained to her that it was a custom among the people with whom she had been living for the past nine years. Uteh understood though she still did not like it. She told Ojebeta to stop it and answer "Eh!" in the usual way when people called her. But Ojebeta found it difficult to eradicate such a long-standing habit, particularly one which had been formed so young; and she became jokingly known as the daughter of Uteh who answered "Mah" and "Sah".

By Ibuza standards, and by the yardstick of her age, Ojebeta was a rich girl. She gave ten shillings of her money to her big mother Uteh to keep for her, and spent three shillings and sixpence to buy gallons of palm oil. On market days a group of them would take their oil across the Niger to the Otu waterside and sell it there for five shillings. They would pay two pennies for the ferry fare, with a shilling they would do *esusu*, a kind of saving, and then they would spend the rest buying soap, fish for their parents, and a head of tobacco for the old people. On Eke days, it was Ojebeta's duty to take all the dirty clothing to the stream to wash it by beating it against the wooden blocks that were there for the purpose.

All in all she was growing into quite a sophisticated young woman of Ibuza who did not have to carry the soul-killing akpu for a living. Sometimes she went to the stream to fetch some akpu as food, but she did not have to sell it to make ends meet. Palm oil selling was not at all a bad occupation. Many people could not afford to take it up since you needed to have a little deposit to buy the oil from the local housewife, to buy your "galawa" which was the empty kerosene tin you put the oil in, and to buy some clean clothes. So palm-oil sellers were a class apart: the very young and the independent, who did not need to make much profit to survive.

Akpu was different. Every farmer practised shifting cultivation; and when a farmer shifted from one farm to a new one, he invariably allowed cassava to grow in the old farm. Cassava thrived in almost any soil, and it did not need tending. The housewife had to go to the farm to dig out the cassava roots, carry the tubers for a mile or so, then soak them in the stream in that part of the water specially divided into squares for women to soak their cassava. It would be left there for three or four days until it was fully fermented and beginning to turn into pulp. Then the housewife would put the pulp into a bag and carry it home, heavy and wet and dripping its milky water. At home, on the night before market day, she would then tie this cassava pulp, still very damp, onto a special akpu basket, piling the basket high with the pulp, securing it with banana strings, and covering the top with smoked banana leaves. Women from Ibuza carrying their akpu to Asaba looked dwarfed under the load of their baskets; some women would even carry two or three of these heavy baskets. After a while the women smelled so much of akpu that you could easily tell a habitual akpu carrier from the more privileged women who traded in palm oil, kernels or lighter commodities like ogili matches and cigarettes. The attraction of akpu was that one needed no deposit; any fool with plenty of energy could do it. There was money in it, too, for you could sell a basket for as much as a shilling in Asaba; so if you carried three or four baskets you had four shillings' gain, just like that.

Soon after Ojebeta arrived in Ibuza she found her age-group; she was told she belonged to "Ogu Aya Okolo" — "Okolo's war". Selling akpu was looked down on as old-fashioned by that group born during Okolo's war. But the older married women retorted, "You will soon be like us," and they were probably right. There was an Ibuza saying that young people think that when they grow up they will reach the sky and touch the stars; but after a while they would realise how far away the sky is.

Ojebeta still maintained her enthusiastic involvement in Christianity. Many Ibuza girls went to the C.M.S. church then, attracted by the songs, especially the translated Ibo songs. Ojebeta was so devout that she was encouraged by the white vicar to attend baptism classes. This was one of the issues that caused minor clashes between her and Uteh and Eze.

Uteh, having watched her for a long time one day doing some kind of sewing with her hands, said: "Ojebeta, what type of man do you think you will marry? You do not know how to farm, and when people call you, you still answer as if you were a goat. Now you start going to this funny place you call church. What is wrong with the religion of your fathers? What is bad in making sacrifices to your dead mother and father and to your personal god?"

Eze stopped lapping up his soup noisily from the wooden bowl his wife had given him, and added, "Oh, she is young. When people are young they think it is something new to be young. Wait until she becomes a woman, that is when you will have to tell her a thing or two. Just be very careful about this new religion, otherwise an old farmer will cut a lock of your hair and you will have to marry him."

"I think, in-law, that is a very bad thing to do to any girl. Suppose I did not wish to marry him? I would like to marry in church and wear a long white dress on the day of my marriage. And I'd like some brass band to play music for me to go to church on the day."

Uteh burst out laughing. "I went to Onitsha some time ago," she said, "and I saw a group of people playing and beating a funny kind of drum, and they were blowing some shiny things — is that what you call brass band? And the young girl in white I saw there, who looked like a ghost and walked like a sleep-walker — was she the new bride? What is wrong with our own music, and our own way of a girl going to her husband's house?"

"It's the work of the devil. The Bible and the Catechism books say so. I must be married in church."

"This church thing does not bother me too much," Eze said by way of compromise. "But if I wanted to go to church I would go to the 'Father' ones. They have more magic, and their outfits when they do their performance resemble those of our head juju priests. They really command respect. And at the end of the performance you are given some alcoholic drink — some people say it is the blood of someone, but those Fathers drink a lot of it. Eh, Ojebeta, why don't you go to that one, instead of the poor one at Umuodafe, where people sing in the Ibo language? The Fathers speak a strange language of the gods. You may not understand it, but you can feel immediately that your *chi* is near when one of the Fathers starts his magical incantations."

"Well, so you have been watching them, have you, Eze? You sound as though you have tasted the drink yourself, the way you talk," Uteh admonished. Then, turning to Ojebeta she said, "It will be difficult for you to find a farmer who would go into all this church stuff with you. Few of our people go to *olu oyibo*, and those who have gone have always taken their wives with them. So you will have to start paying attention to those young farmers who come to meet you on your way from Asaba."

So afraid was Ojebeta that all she had learned at Ma Palagada's would be wasted that she prayed to God to send her an Ibuza man who had experience of the white man's work and would know the value of what she had learned.

Meanwhile she and some of her friends still looked down on the other age-groups who carried akpu and who did not go to church; and even before they were baptised they all found it fashionable to take European names. So Ogbanje Ojebeta added the English name of Alice. Now if you called her just Ogbanje, or just Ojebeta, she would not answer; but if you said Ogbanje Alice, she would flash her snow-white teeth at you and greet you. It became a common type of occurrence in Ibuza at that time among those who wanted to show how modern they were. It was a little comical when even young people who did not go to church took on names so exotic to them that they could not even pronounce them. So you might hear a girl saying her names were "Kilisi, Ngbeke" — "Christy", coupled uneasily with her original Ibo name which meant "born on Eke day". The trend reached such a pass that people became shy of their native Ibuza names.

The irony was that the process would eventually come full circle and people would reject their English names; but that was to be in the days of Independence, after the end of colonialism. That was still in the future.

14 Arrival of a Stranger

Sunday morning had become one of the most colourful times in Ibuza. It was then that you could see everybody rushing about: the pagans going to their farms, some market women hurrying to their stalls, the young set embracing various kinds of Christianity, going to Umuodafe if they believed in worship according to the Church of England, or towards Afieke if they liked the brand of Roman Catholicism brought to Ibuza by the Irish priests and their nuns.

There was no specific time for church. Some of the very early Catholics went for communion as soon as the late cock had ended its morning crowing; that particular mass was a very important duty for those who attended it, mostly the very old and the school-boys. But when it came to the later mass, usually round nine o'clock, when the sun was out, everybody took the opportunity to display their latest lappa and show the world that they belonged to the church.

On this particular Sunday, which fell on Eke day, Alice Ogbanje Ojebeta, as she now liked to be called, went to the stream early, bathed and rubbed her skin with coconut oil which she had scented with the new flower perfume she had bought from a Hausa hawker in Asaba. The scent was so pleasant that on her way back friends and relatives kept asking for a little of her "oil or soap or whatever it is you have used to make you smell so nice". She gave a drop to this person, another drop to that one; it was a good thing she had taken only a small amount with her, having by now learned the habit of her people. They had sweet stories of hardship to tell any-body who cared to listen, all to get something out of you. When she came across Ukabegwu's young daughter she handed her the whole bottle which was by then almost empty, but she asked that she might have the bottle returned, for she had had it since the time she was in Onitsha.

She thought nostalgically of her stay at Otu Onitsha sometimes, especially of Amanna and the others, though she was in no doubt of the fact that she would rather stay in Ibuza where she was wanted by her people and where she was regarded as the daughter of an illustrious man. In a sense she was still not free now, for no woman or girl in Ibuza was free, except those who committed the abominable sin of prostitution or those who had been completely cast off or rejected by their people for offending one custom or another. A girl was owned, in particular, by her father or someone in place of her father or her older brother, and then, in general, by her group or homestead. But at least she belonged to these people by right of birth, and nobody would dare to call her slave because she was not.

Sometimes Ojebeta thought of Clifford, then dismissed him quickly from her mind. Admittedly she had felt slightly abandoned at first at his apparent loss of interest, but she now realised that in fact she was thankful the proposed match had so far come to nothing. In Ibuza, despite the fact that the final choice of a husband for a girl was made by her people she was free to protest in private, and if she came from a good family, where money was not the be-all and end-all, they would listen to her and make some adjustments as to the man in question. In most cases you knew the man beforehand, especially if he was a farmer, and the two of you would have been allowed to amuse yourselves together in the evenings and on moonlit nights. Ojebeta knew that according to the new Christian religion it was against God's will to allow young boys or prospective husbands to fondle you and indulge in the exhaustive type of romance Ibuza boys played with you; but that was the custom of her people, and the only way one's future husband was able to tell if a girl was sympathetic, shy, able to bear pain, and comforting. She, like all girls of her age, was encouraged to subject herself to this kind of heavy flirtation, though she must never allow a man his way completely. A girl who lost her virginity before marriage was better dead. But at least here Ojebeta had the freedom to enjoy herself as well. With Clifford it would have been a command marriage. She was happy she had not fallen for it, she rationalised now, and been tempted to remain at Otu.

"Our Olisa forbid," her aunt Uteh had sworn when Ojebeta told her what might have happened had she stayed there just a day longer. "It was the spirit of your dead parents guiding you home. About Okolie and the money he got for you — do not speak of it, for it is a thing too shameful. I know you will marry well, a sympathetic man who will repay the money. Now I see why Okolie never made any way in life, and never will make any. Your dead father would never forgive him for committing that kind of an atrocity. With all that money, Okolie could not make it here as a farmer, and his wife is still waiting for him in her parents' house. They have no children. He is in Lagos now, a burden to your big brother Owezim and his wife. They say he cannot hold down a job. I would not be surprised if we see him back sometime in the near future."

She sighed, then fixed Ojebeta with a look from her dark brown eyes that were heavily lined with *otangele*. There was no sense in being anything but philosophical about the situation. "No woman is ever free. To be owned by a man is a great honour. So perhaps in a sense your brother was not too much in the wrong. He only took the money that by right belonged to the first son of the family, Owezim — he alone, and not Okolie, has the right to sell you, or borrow money on your head, or spend your bride price. So you must forgive Okolie. For he will be able to defend you if you marry a nasty husband. If you have brothers behind you, the man will respect you the more and will be frightened to treat you badly. So forget the past. Such things do happen."

Ojebeta did not need this latter admonishment at all. She was happy to be free, to enjoy her people, to watch her small savings grow, to go with her age-group and friends to the big market to select the abada material to buy for this celebration or that one.

When they had collected their first *esusu* savings about a year ago, a few months after she had left Onitsha, she had determined to cross over to Otu market to see her former friends; but they had been driven back by people who said there was a really big riot going on in Aba, that most of the cloth stalls in Otu Onitsha had been looted, that many white people had been killed and that those Onitsha market women who had been secretly supporting the white people had been brought to justice and their stalls demolished. Something inside Ojebeta told her that the Palagada family must be affected somehow, and this belief became more entrenched as the months went by and Clifford did not show up. It was not that she looked forward to his coming for her — in fact she was haunted by the prospect — but the more time passed, the less likely it became that he would come. The mere thought of being free to marry someone from Ibuza added to her happiness.

She was full of this happiness on her way from the stream that

158

Sunday morning. She quickly warmed the food left over from the previous evening and ate it with gusto, for walking up and down the hill to the stream could be extremely tiring, especially if you went before the morning meal. She heard the first peals of the church bells as she was washing up the iron pots and humming some choruses of the new hymns she had learned by heart. This was one of the privileges she enjoyed most, the freedom to be able to sing whenever she felt like it and not be inhibited by the fact that she might wake someone up. There was something very special about this Sunday. First, she had been able to acquire a complete new abada outfit, after more than nine months of saving. Then there was the coincidence of it being Eke day as well. Very few Sundays fell on the days of the greatest market they had in Ibuza, so such days were days of double festivities. She would go to the church, then pay a visit to her people in Umuisagba, then walk round the market enjoying the dances performed by different groups of people, buying a bit of *otangele* for her eyes here, a bit of washing soap there, and just walking round and saying hello to almost everybody. She loved to hear people ask, "Is that not the daughter of Okwuekwu Oda, whose parents died during the felenza?" and she, flashing her white teeth at them, would answer, "Yes, I am their daughter." In Ibuza there were very few strangers.

On this Eke Sunday, Ojebeta put on her new clothes, brushed her Ibo hymn book and Bible until the covers shone and then tied the two together with the special Sunday handkerchief she had made for herself. She had another white handkerchief in her hand, holding only the tip of it so that its full beauty would not be missed as she made her way to her friend's hut to tell her that it was time for church, and had she not heard the church bell ringing.

Uteh and her husband admired her, saying, "You look beautiful enough to marry the Oba of Idu."

Ojebeta laughed and set out proudly on her way, only to meet the friend she had been going to fetch.

"Ifenkili Angelina!" she cried with joy. "I was just coming to your house."

"But so was I to yours, Ojebeta Alice."

By the time they reached Afia Eke on their way to the church they had formed into a sparkling group, proud to be young and happy in their youth. In church, those who like Ojebeta could read were the choir girls and would start the songs, to the arm-flingings of the school teacher.

159

There was some excitement in the church today. Ojebeta could not find out the reason for it since the music teacher, who was also the pastor, was already there waiting for the church to fill before starting. As she hurried to her place Ojebeta noticed a seated man who exchanged a few whispered words with the pastor. She could see from his European style that this unfamiliar person was from *olu oyibo*. He was very dark and he was wearing a white shirt, a tie and a jacket, and had a pair of spectacles like one of the white men at Otu. Ojebeta was impressed, for her long stay with the Palagadas had taught her to appreciate such foreign clothes. To concentrate on her singing became a herculean task, for she kept wondering: *Have our people really become so civilised? So is that how life is in the white men's jobs in those far away places?*

Her curiosity was soon allayed when the pastor told them: "My brothers and sisters, it is not every day we have the honour of being visited by one of our successful sons from the big cities. We now have such a person here — Jacob Okonji. He was trained by Bishop Onyeaboh, the great bishop of the whole Niger, before going to work in Lagos. He is here now to visit us, and he will read us the word of God."

It became clear that Jacob Okonji was not a great talker. He simply stood up, confidently surveyed the congregation in front of him, smiled briefly and said: "My brothers and sisters, welcome. I am happy to be with you and that we praise God together. . . ." Then he went straight on to the text.

He was a good reader, an educated man, though he stammered a great deal and Ojebeta felt sorry for him. She had surmised that he was of medium height when she had first seen him seated, and she was right; he was also thin, with a soft voice and manners. After the service was over, it was customary for half the congregation, or even the whole congregation, to stay and talk to any newcomer; many would simply go to his home village and visit him there instead.

"Let's not bother to crowd round him," said Angelina. "We'll go to his family hut."

"Do you know him?" asked Ojebeta tentatively.

"Yes, he came home three years ago, on his way to Lagos to look for work. This is his first visit since getting his job. He's very smart. They call him Jacob the Whiteman because he behaves and acts mildly like a white man."

"He gave the church a huge contribution last harvest," another

160

girl in the group added. "He sent the money through another C.M.S. member who was living in Lagos."

"I didn't know we had such people in our town," said Ojebeta.

"Oh, yes, we do. Wait till you see some of the really rich families and their wives when they come home on leave. They all have supple bodies, since they no longer have to carry akpu even for cooking! I'd like to go to *olu oyibo* too, to get away from this place," Angelina Ifenkili sighed.

The others laughed, reminding her that many were called but few were chosen: not everyone who went to Lagos and the big cities in the country of the Hausas always struck it rich. Rebecca told the story of a relative of hers who had gone to one of those far places and been employed as a washerman, like most illiterate Ibuza people there at the time; she said they had been so poor that when the wife washed her only lappa she would have to stay indoors until it dried, before being able to go out to market to fetch food for her family.

"I have heard of some who couldn't get jobs at all and had to come back home and be farmers."

They agreed that it was so, and that as God had taught them they should be content with their lot.

When they came to Umuodafe, the village of the newcomer from Lagos, there were already several people waiting to welcome him. He soon arrived from the church, and instead of serving his visitors with only kolanut and alligator pepper he gave them some very tasty biscuits. The last time Ojebeta had eaten biscuits like that had been at Ma's wake; her friends saved some to take home to their parents, and so did she.

Jacob went round greeting them all one by one and enquiring who they were. When he came to Ojebeta and asked her who she was, she told him she had a brother by the name of Owezim, who also lived in Lagos, with his wife.

"Oh, I know them well," replied Jacob, "very well. They live on the island and I live on the mainland, but we meet every month at the Ibuza meeting." Regular reunions with those from the same community were a strong feature of Ibo life among those who had left home, wherever they travelled.

"Are they well?" Ojebeta asked concerned.

"Oh, yes, they were quite well when I saw them last, about a month ago. Your brother's wife is from my village, you know, so we are in-laws. But they never told me that they had an educated

161

and well brought-up pretty young girl like you at all. In fact coming back to Ibuza is always an eye-opener."

"Thank you very much. I was away for a long time," Ojebeta said, moving away slightly. She was beginning to feel embarrassed, for this stranger looked as if he was likely to spend the whole afternoon asking her about herself. How could one tell such a person that one's own brother had sent one away because he wanted money for his Uloko dance and for his yam seeds? Luckily, the pastor called Jacob away, and they all grouped together in the compound of Jacob's older brother and sang some church choruses.

More biscuits were distributed, and the adults drank some palm wine. Then they had to leave, for more relatives were coming to greet the new arrival and see if he had brought any presents for them or any news from Lagos. In those days there were few post offices and those that did exist were too unreliable to trust; so if you were in Lagos and were planning a visit home, you told all your people during the monthly family meeting. Through you people would send anything from money to small parcels; you could hardly refuse anyone without really offending that person and causing everyone to think you selfish, nor did you charge one another for such services, knowing that it could be your turn next. So the family of a visitor would have to be ready to receive callers right up until the time the visitor was about to depart again, taking foodstuffs back for various people in Lagos.

Jacob did not waste much time in tracking down where Ojebeta lived, for he had only two weeks' leave from his employment as an apprentice moulder in the new railway foundry. He was an élite among his people because he could read and write; he did not have to take work as a house servant, a washerman or a mere labourer. He was now confident in his job, because it had a future, it was permanent, and there would be a kind of pension at the end of it. To achieve all this had taken him quite a long time.

He had assisted Bishop Onyeaboh as a servant for over twelve years, before the latter decided that some kind of education would prepare him for his future life. He had been twenty when he started school and, because he was a keen scholar and because of the discipline he had learned in the house of the Bishop, his five years' education served him then as if he had been to a modern university. He achieved what was then known as Standard Six, and would have gone into clerical work, starting as a messenger, had he not been advised to learn a trade since that would have more security. He

162

was soon employed as an apprentice: the Bishop's glowing recommendation was enough to convince the colonial masters who ran the railways of Nigeria that this was a young person of a new breed. He had not disappointed them.

Now that he was approaching thirty, when most of his age-group who were farmers already had several children and some of them several wives, he found himself looking for a girl to marry. He had come home to look round, and would have settled for any intelligent farmer's daughter, as long as the girl would become a Christian and was prepared to be married in church. But from what he had seen that Sunday morning he knew he would have no difficulty in finding his choice. Being a naturally shy person, and also aware that he was no longer young and that his leave was a very short one, he began making enquiries about Ojebeta from his people soon after she had left. He was not at all displeased with what he heard about her. He kept thinking how wise it was of her people to send Ojebeta away to her rich relative to be trained the modern way, when many people would have preferred to keep such a girl at home to help them run their farm. "It simply goes to show how discerning some people are," he said to himself. "And her two brothers in Lagos, not mentioning it at all — it just shows...."

Jacob paid Ojebeta a visit with his young nephew, his brother's only son who was almost twenty years of age, though still at school (in those days even some married men went to school, to qualify themselves for the new wave of jobs that was taking many farmers away from their farms to the crowding cities and towns). Jacob and his nephew were well received by Uteh and her husband, and Ojebeta entertained them with kolanuts and some fresh green fruits. They talked generally, then after a while Uteh and her husband began to see the way the conversation was going and realised that Jacob had not come to visit them as fellow Ibuza citizens: he was interested in knowing more about Ojebeta.

Jacob felt very happy on their way home. He really liked her. "Such an intelligent girl," he remarked thoughtfully to his nephew.

"Yes, the only girl we have who can read in Ibo and do some very nice needlework. She is well trained, and I like her."

It soon became a habit for Jacob to visit Ojebeta every evening. After only a week Ojebeta could not think of a time when she did not have Jacob on her mind. Then one night he asked her whether she would like him to ask her people if they approved of him.

"They are not really my people—Eze is only my in-law. But they could make things very difficult for you if they do not like you."

"But, Ojebeta, do you like me? Do you love me? I would like to marry you if your people will accept me."

"I would too — but of course the decision rests with my big brother in Lagos. He owns the money for my head."

"I'll have to talk to him," he concluded, hesitantly touching her. He had been so disciplined that he thought of himself as being out of practice with the opposite sex, and especially the younger members.

She did not push him away or laugh him off, as he had thought she might, but let his hand stay on her shoulder. He pulled her gently to him, letting her head rest on his shoulder.

"I'm in such a hurry. And my time is very short. Can we convince your big mother Uteh to let you go to Lagos with me? I shall take care of you and will settle the bride price there, and we will send Uteh's share to her through people coming home."

It suddenly seemed to Ojebeta that all her life she had been waiting for this person. He was so comforting, so reassuring. *So this is how it is all going to end,* she thought. *Me marrying this civilised person, who even bothered to ask me if I like him, and me going to Lagos to see my two brothers, and then having a home of my own, all at once?* She felt like crying at least to relieve the painful happiness, but she could not. There were so many things she wanted to tell him — but where could she start? It would be such a long story.

Instead she nodded like a dumb person, trusting him completely. Yes, she would like to go with him, she would.

Only how would they convince Uteh and her husband Eze?

15 Slave with a New Master

Uteh and her husband resented the suggestion of Ojebeta leaving them. It was Eze who proved the most difficult.

"No," he maintained, "Ojebeta is not going to Lagos, not if I can prevent it. The poor girl has only been back in Ibuza two years. She still has to learn many of our ways; and then somebody in trousers instead of a loin cloth comes to snatch her away, right here under our very noses. No, she is not going. How do we know the man is not a wife beater? How do we know he has no peculiar diseases? What do we know about him?"

In a way it was quite comical, not just because Eze was an in-law who normally should have had little or no say in Ojebeta's future but because it was Eze with his watery eyes and stooped back who was wanting to know about someone else's defects. But Ojebeta had learned to keep her thoughts to herself. She knew that since she was an orphan, with no brothers or sisters near her, everybody, good or bad, healthy or maimed, would have pieces of advice for her in plenty. She smiled through it all, agreeing with everyone.

She learned of one of the reasons why Eze was so against her marrying Jacob by sheer accident one night. They had all gone to their sleeping places. Uteh and Eze were lying on the wide couch near the fire, which was still very alive, glowing and lighting their faces. It was a fairly chilly night, for the season of the harmattan wind was fast approaching.

Ojebeta was on the other side of the open room. She was young so did not need any fire; she had wrapped herself in one of the old lappas she used for sleeping in, and lay on a soft mat she had brought from Onitsha, thinking about everything — how her brother Okolie had abandoned her, and how that might now lead to a good ending. She felt strangely close to Okolie still, remembering his warmth when she had been a child and how he would carry her on his shoulders to the farm on those few occasions he ventured there. The human mind being what it is, she did not remember the agony she had suffered when he had left her in Otu market, though she remembered the humiliation she had experienced on first being called a slave; she did not remember how very alone she had felt when she had had her identity charms brutally cut away from her. All she knew was that because Okolie had taken her to Otu to be trained, Jacob now wanted her to be his wife; for that she was thankful.

She even blamed providence for what she had done to Okolie. She knew that he was still not gainfully employed, though it was six years since he had left Ibuza. Sometimes she had entertained thoughts of having him back in Ibuza, so that things would be as they had been before she went to Onitsha. She could not will her parents back, since one of death's cruelties was that it was so final; but her brother Okolie — how she longed to see him again, to tell him of the fearful joy she was feeling about Jacob, to hear from him that she was doing the right thing, to feel his care, to listen to his voice. . . . Then she stopped thinking about herself and her brother, for she could hear an argument heating up between Uteh and her husband.

They must have been talking for a while, but she had been too wrapped up in her own thoughts to hear them. Now their voices were like a rising song that started with a low tune and gained in volume till it was raised to the highest pitch. They seemed oblivious of the fact that Ojebeta might still be awake and might hear them speaking their thoughts aloud. They had been so carried away by the intensity of the argument that it was no longer possible for Ojebeta to do anything but listen.

"Why don't you want her to go? Why, why are you so against it? Many people make a great deal of money there, you know. . . ."

"Yes," laughed Eze, his voice sounding like that of a hoarse frog, "yes, so did your nephew Okolie. He was going there to get rich in a day, and we still haven't seen him. His wife is still not paid for — the poor woman sits wasting her life waiting for her husband to make big money. . . ."

Ojebeta could hear the rustling of mats as Uteh got up, now incensed. She raised her voice to its highest, not caring if Ojebeta heard or not.

"Leave Okolie out of it! It's only that he met with misfortune, that's all. His brother Owezim isn't such a failure, is he? He has a good job, a house full of boys of his own — why don't you talk of him, and leave Okolie out of it? In any case, what have our people got to do with this man Jacob from Umuodafe? He isn't a failure either, you can see that. What is behind all this? I have never seen you worked up about something that it not your business before."

"I don't care what you say, whether it is my business or not. I have seen Ojebeta blossom into a young woman. She is not leaving this village, she is marrying my cousin. . . . All those things, all that learning wasted, to go away from us, just because this Jacob wears trousers. . . ."

"What cousin are you talking about, Eze?"

"My cousin Adim. He will make her a good husband. He is a strong man, works hard and has not been married before. Ojebeta would be his first wife."

"Oh," Uteh said, now subdued. "Yes, Adim is a good man, but why did he not speak up before? Why wait all this long time until Jacob comes from Lagos to win Ojebeta's heart?"

"He's saving for the bride price. He said he would pay part of it to Ukabegwu after the yam festival, when he will be free to sell some of his harvest."

"I don't think Ojebeta will like him, because he does not go to sing in the church of the C.M.S. people."

"Well, we all know what a man can do to a girl to make her his wife for ever. . . ."

Uteh's voice which had been returning to normal rose again to screaming point at this. Ojebeta was sure they would come to blows on her account.

"What are you talking about? Cut a curl of Ojebeta's hair? You are wicked, Eze — to think I have been living and sleeping with a man who could entertain such an idea in his head, and to think you would want to do a thing like that to my only female relative, Ojebeta the only daughter of Umeadi and Okwuekwu Oda. . . . Oh, you are wicked!"

Ojebeta was so shaken by what she had overheard, by the mere suggestion of this monstrous ploy, that she jumped up from where she had been lying and dreaming and stood quaking like African water lilies on a windy day. Suddenly the whole issue of her own future seemed dependent on stopping the two angry voices and the violence that threatened to erupt between Uteh and Eze at any moment. If only to gain time to think, she knew she had to intervene, to tell the two quarrelling adults not to mind so much on her

167

behalf, to calm them, even to lie to them and say she did not mind marrying Eze's relative — oh, to say anything that would take the sting, the pain out of it all, at least for a while. Recovering from the shock, she managed to assure them laughingly — how faked that laughter was! — that everything would be all right, that she was not committed to Jacob anyway.

Somehow Eze and Uteh settled their differences after that, and soon went back to sleep.

But not Ojebeta. Her night was ruined. She had been a slave before against her wishes; if this time she must marry and belong to a man according to the custom of her people, she intended doing so with her eyes wide open. She had no parents to choose for her; the decision would probably lie with her brothers in Lagos. However she intended having a say in the matter. She sneaked to where Eze kept his shaving knife and shaved off every last vestige of hair on her head, then went out to the back of the hut and burned all the pieces. It upset her to do this, for she had been proud of her jet black hair which she had never been allowed to grow as she wanted at Ma Palagada's; the Otu barber had kept their hair very closely trimmed, though when it became apparent that she was being kept for Clifford she had been allowed to grow her hair a few inches. Since she had been back in Ibuza she had even indulged in plaiting her hair and she really looked forward to Eke days when she usually had it washed and re-plaited.

Now she had lost it all. Like her *ogbanje* charms, her hair seemed to symbolise her freedom. Would she ever be free? Must she be a slave all her life, never being allowed to do what she liked? Was it the fate of all Ibuza women or just her own? Still it would have been better to be a slave to a master of your choice, than to one who did not care or even know who you were. Jacob would be a better choice, especially if her brothers in Lagos should happen to approve of him.

Jacob's one big fault, as Ojebeta had come to realise in just a few days of knowing him, was that he was a very conventional person and would do nothing that went against custom, tradition or local mores. "No," he kept saying to her, "your people must approve of your husband. Have you ever heard of a marriage succeeding without the parents' consent to it?" That was why Ojebeta was all the more surprised when after she had told him of what she had overheard Eze saying Jacob heaved a great sigh, and said:

"I think the best thing is what we decided before: I shall take

168

you to your brothers in Lagos. But as things are now you have to be quiet about it and say nothing to your big mother Uteh."

Ojebeta's immediate reaction was to be cautious in her excitement, for this bold decision was quite uncharacteristic of Joseph. Then it came to her that this must indeed be proof of the depth of his feelings for her and, overjoyed, she agreed to the plan. She was anxious, however, about Uteh. "She'll be brokenhearted and will miss me so. Who will help her with the fetching and carrying of water?"

"Don't worry about it. I will send her a message as soon as we have left, through my people. As for fetching and carrying water, you would have to leave her sometime, wouldn't you? Even if you married a farmer, you would not be able to do all that for her any longer, because your husband would surely need you on his farm."

The next Nkwo day, when Ojebeta and all her friends were taking their palm oil to Asaba to sell, was very wet. Yet despite the weather many people from Jacob's side of Ibuza turned out to bid him goodbye. His nephew carried his wooden box, and two other women carried his bags of presents and books and some Ibuza farm produce. They trotted in the rain most of the time like horses, holding lively conversations at the same time. They soon caught up with the group of girls going to Asaba who, though they were walking fast, could not match the rapid pace of Jacob and his carriers, who were mainly men. The girls, knowing that they would be dry as soon as the sun came out, did not in the meantime mind getting wet. In fact the cool rain was refreshing, and seemed to be washing all dirt from the leaves by the wayside, from the ground and from their bodies. They seemed to be walking in a cleaner world, thanks to the rain.

When Jacob's group caught up with them, Ifenkili Angelina said laughingly, "So you are going back today?"

"Yes," Jacob replied, mopping the rain water from his brow. It was quite a heavy downpour, the type that would stop in less than an hour, though to wait for it to stop would mean missing his mammy-wagon. "I have to go back now, otherwise the white people will cut my food money." He laughed lightly.

"We wish you luck, and safe journey — may you not meet with any accidents," the girls chorused. "We hope you'll make more and more money to come home and give to your people."

He nodded and said "Amen" — not *Ise* as he would have said had he never left Ibuza.

169

He cast only one glance at Ojebeta, and walked fast with the people carrying his belongings.

At the end of that market day, which though it had started with such a downpour was now quite dry, Ifenkili Angelina went to a friend of theirs and asked: "Do you know, I've been to the stall that Ojebeta was fond of occupying and she isn't there. I don't even know if she sold her tin of palm oil. I asked her customer from the east if Ojebeta had sold him her palm oil and he told me he had waited the whole day for her and because she hadn't turned up he had to buy his oil from another girl. In fact he was packing and getting ready to go back to Otu when I saw him."

"Then what can have happened to her?" Rebecca Mbeke wondered. "She couldn't have been taken ill and gone home without telling us, could she? We will have to look for her. You had better call the other girls when they are ready. I'm just going to the waterside to rinse my tin and then I will join you in the search."

"Yes, and if you find her, tell her we're waiting for her and that she should hurry."

Rebecca Mbeke wondered what Ojebeta would be doing at the waterside for her to find her there; but maybe Angelina was just worried and confused. Was there not a saying that a mother who has lost her child finds fault in everything and everybody?

At the end of the day, when they had looked high and low for Ojebeta, and concluded that either she had gone home without telling them or that sometthing was drastically the matter with her, it was with heavy hearts and unhappy faces that the girls set off for Ibuza.

Instead of going to their different homes, when they returned, they went to tell Ojebeta's aunt Uteh what had happened. It was with great surprise that they were told that Ojebeta had gone to Lagos, and for good, and that she had gone with Jacob, who had sent his people to inform them not to worry. But Uteh was worrying, and not simply worrying: she was taking steps to get Ojebeta back.

They were sending someone to Asaba the very next morning to send an urgent telegram to intercede all mammy-wagons that had left Asaba the day Ojebeta and Jacob had set out for Lagos. Eze assured the bewildered girls that he himself would be following the special learned messenger to Asaba. They were sure they would get her back the following day. Everyone then went home feeling somewhat relieved.

170

In those days the journey from Ibuza to Lagos took four days. There were so many stopping places on the way, and the mammy-wagons needed a lot of fuel, fixing and pushings to make them work. They stopped at Warri, Benin, Ifo, Ibadan and then finally arrived at Lagos. At Benin and Ibadan, the passengers stopped and rested for the night.

Ojebeta had never in her life been packed in so tightly with other humans before. Not only did they have to cope with the smells from other people, they also had to share the same airless wagon with dried fish, meat, cloth and even live hens. At first she was worried and not a little scared; but after a short rest at Agbor, during which time she was refreshed with the clear water from the stream, her spirit stopped flagging. At Benin, Jacob, accustomed to much travelling, had bargained for a comfortable sleeping place for both of them. He assured her that she was doing the right thing, that there was bound to come a time when she would have to leave her people, leave Uteh and leave Ibuza. Had she not been trained in the European way? For a girl like her Ibuza was too parochial. In Lagos, if her brothers approved of him, they would have a white wedding; she would never have to go to the farm, she would live as she used to at Ma Palagada's, but with this difference: it would be her own home and her own children she would be looking after.

As gently as he had assured her, he told her the story of his life. He told her that he had had to leave home in search of a white man's job because there had been a great famine in Ibuza at the time, and his brother — the father of his young nephew who had seen them off at Asaba — had started finding fault with everything he did. It had come to a climax one day when in his childish forgetfulness Jacob had left the piece of yam they were going to eat on the farm for too long in the fire: the yam was burnt and they had little left for their midday meal. His brother was murderously annoyed. Jacob laughed bitterly at the recollection of it, and absent-mindedly squeezed Ojebeta's hand. She could tell it had been a painful experience for young boy of Jacob's age at the time.

"I was chased out of the farm with a raised cutlass — in those days you could kill and get away with it. I still carry the scar where the cutlass grazed my upper arm. I didn't wait for my brother to strike another blow. I ran for my life."

"And yet you came back and stayed in his big hut?" Ojebeta was beginning to understand the type of man she would be calling her husband in a few months' time.

171

Jacob laughed again and said by way of reply: "I became a Christian, and I survived it all." He added after a short while, "Anyway it all happened a very long time ago, when my brother was in his heyday. Now he is silver headed; and we are brothers."

Ojebeta realised that he must have been very lucky to be alive at all, for the forests of those days were full of wild animals, lions, and elephants (which were yet to be exterminated for their tusks); lucky to have escaped the greatest danger of all, the head-hunters in and around Benin. At one stage of his escape Jacob had been caught by one of the right-hand men of the Benin king Akenzua, and had been invited to watch the executions of some highway robbers who had killed innocent people in a nearby village. It was at this same time that the Bishop Onyeaboh came to visit the Oba of Benin, and they had given Jacob to him as a gift, for like the Bishop he was Ibo.

"So," Ojebeta finalised, "we are both orphans."

"Yes," agreed Jacob. "We have both lost our parents. When we are married you shall be my mother, and I hope to live up to the role of father to you."

"I hope so," said Ojebeta in a very small voice. She prayed quietly that her brothers would have no reason to disqualify Jacob. He was so gentle. He was of medium height, not tall like the people in her family; but he was so polished that he never made any rude remarks, even in jest. One could see that he had been taught to think before he spoke, and this combined with his stammer to make him a very quiet man indeed. He would sit for hours with her, without saying a word though being eloquent enough in his behaviour towards her.

It was when they had been fully refreshed by the night's sleep that a messenger from the local post office came to their wagon asking for a certain Alice Ojebeta. Instinctively Ojebeta wanted to answer to her name, but so deep was the trust and respect she had for this man Jacob that when he signalled to her with his eyes to be silent she complied without question. When no one responded, the messenger went running to the next mammy-wagon, to continue the search for an Alice Ogbanje Ojebeta who had to be called back home to Ibuza.

After many months of arguments, discussions and negotiations with her family, Jacob's wishes did indeed come true. He married

172

Ojebeta, and she became his wife and took the extra title of Mrs Okonji, which her people translated to "Misisi". It was so difficult for them to comprehend these foreign beliefs that they had sub- jected Ojebeta to something of an interrogation when the whole ceremony of church and white wedding was over. They wanted to know why it was essential for her to go to a church and have those strange foreign words said over her, just because she was going to her husband's house, when anyway all the native prayers had al- ready been said, all the necessary sacrifices had been made to her dead parents and to the Oboshi River goddess of Ibuza, and the bride price had been paid.

Mrs Ogbanje Ojebeta Alice Okonji, the daughter of Okwue- kwu Oda, had herself been confused and could only reply to such puzzled questions: "Well, it is like a man cutting a lock of a girl's hair — it makes a marriage last forever until either of them dies. But unlike the cutting of the hair, the husband is restricted too. He has to marry only me, just one wife as the Bible says."

"Suppose you did not have children for him, what would he do? What would his people say to you, holding their son like that?"

Ojebeta did not know the answer to that one. (But years later Nigerian men solved the problem by themselves. A woman could be taken to church and a ring slipped on her finger — as easily as a piece of string can be put round a man's cattle to mark it out from another person's. But that did not mean the man could have only her. What if he had enough money to afford more wives, or if the first one married in church had no child? So men would simply take wives when they felt like it; while women, on the other hand, must have one husband, and only one. But only a stupid woman would expect her husband to remain married to her alone. What was she, if not only a woman?)

Nonetheless, before long Ojebeta did start having children for her husband. One does not ask whether they loved and cared for each other ever after; those words make no sense in a situation like this. There was certainly a kind of eternal bond between husband and wife, a bond produced maybe by centuries of traditions, taboos and, latterly, Christian dogma. Slave, obey your master. Wife, honour your husband, who is your father, your head, your heart, your soul. So there was little room for Ojebeta to exercise her own individuality, her own feelings, for these were entwined in Jacob's. She was lucky, however, that although Jacob proved to be quite a jealous man he was above all a Christian. In her own way, Ojebeta

173

was content and did not want more of life; she was happy in her husband, happy to be submissive, even to accept an occasional beating, because that was what she had been brought up to believe a wife should expect. For his part, Jacob worked hard and was a good provider.

One thing still worried them. Okolie had finally confessed that he had actually sold his sister for eight pounds, and that according to the custom she remained legally Palagada property. This realisation was painful to Jacob, and he knew that debt must be paid somehow, for their own peace of mind. It was not the kind of thing one wanted other people to know about: one had to do it under cover, because it was a shameful thing. Owezim had reprimanded and remonstrated with his younger brother Okolie in a profusion of bad language, perhaps beginning somewhat to blame himself for having left home so early. But despite the recriminations, the harm had already been done. Jacob had not known the full truth until after the wedding; neither had Owezim been quite aware that Ojebeta's stay at Otu was the result of this precise financial transaction. For the time being they all decided to keep quiet about the situation, until it could be respectably resolved, and they prayed that in the meantime nothing untoward would happen.

After three years, Ojebeta had given birth to a baby girl, then a boy, and there had been no problems; it seemed she had so far escaped the doom forecast for unredeemed slaves. But then trouble indeed started: she began to lose her babies, and Jacob's mind went to the issue of Ma Palagada's money. He prayed to God many, many times yet his prayers went unanswered. So he and Ojebeta in desperation consulted a dibia in Lagos and this native medicine man confirmed their suspicion; he assured them that Ma's son Clifford was alive and would before long approach them to claim his eight pounds back.

Meanwhile, Ojebeta miscarried again and Jacob was frantic with worry.

At Otu, Ma Palagada had created a bigger cloth empire than those she left behind could sustain. None of these people — her daughters, her husband, her son — could afford to keep a house full of servants, and the likelihood was that the family would be jettisoned back into obscurity. Her name might still be seen engraved on church walls in Otu, or carved on some expensive tombstone; but the reality was that the direct Palagada line was reduced to simply a common individual. Clifford had been unable to make a success of his business dealings either. Everything seemed to have disintegrated since Ma's death. In his mood of disillusionment he saw no reason why he should go to Ibuza to look for Ojebeta, on whom he was no longer keen anyway. She had too many tribal marks on her face to warrant his making such a journey. He could hardly recall what he could ever have found attractive in such a slave girl.

"But what of your money?" Pa asked. "Your mother paid for the girl; she belongs to this family."

Clifford could not dispute that.

As the years passed he needed all the more whatever money he could lay his hands on, to help himself and to help care for his half-brothers — four of them his father had had with Chiago. Pa Palagada was ageing fast, and Clifford knew that the task of bringing up those boys would eventually fall on his shoulders. Business at Otu was too precarious for such a responsibility; he needed a regular income, and he must certainly recover all the monies owed to his mother.

Eventually he joined the army (luckily for him the British needed every pair of hands to lend support to the big war they were fighting in Europe). It was on one of his home leaves that he traced Ojebeta to Lagos, and at once he sent a message there that he would be coming to see them. Without more being said, it was understood by all that he was coming for his money.

Okolie pleaded with Jacob, saying that he had spent the eight pounds many years before, and was not in a position to refund it. Owezim, with so many family burdens of his own, was just not able to afford the amount, though he felt sorry for Jacob since he had already parted with the required bride price. Both his brothers-in-law were apologetic and sympathetic. However the message was clear to Jacob. Ojebeta was his wife, the children that were dying were his, so if he wanted to have things running smoothly within his own household he would now have to pay for it.

It was with open arms that they welcomed Clifford, immaculate in his brown khaki uniform, and much surprised that he was being treated as an important person in Ojebeta's home. He had expected her husband to be at least aggressive, if not openly unfriendly, but instead he was greeted with:

"Welcome, welcome. You are the people responsible for my present happiness and pride." Jacob talked nervously, contrary to

175

his nature. "Ojebeta, Ojebeta! Our guest has arrived. Clifford the son of Ma is here. Come and welcome him."

Ojebeta rushed in from the backyard kitchen where she had been preparing a chicken stew specially for Clifford's visit. She rubbed the edge of her lappa over her shiny nose, then pulled the lappa tight round her still narrow waist.

Clifford stood there completely dumb with astonishment.

Ojebeta had changed. She was thinner, much older than his imagination would have allowed. She was also very nervous, and rather unsure of herself and her unbecoming outfit. He could still glimpse the ghost of the girl he had known so many years ago, in the carriage of the neck and in the jet black skin that still shone in places. But the old Ojebeta — the energetic, laughing one — was gone forever. He wanted to end this business and clear out of her life once and for all. Momentarily he wondered what had happened to change her so much?

To Ojebeta, Clifford looked much younger. He held himself rather straight and stiff, as all army people seemed to, but this erectness gave him the appearance of extra tallness — somehow he seemed to have stretched. His boots and his military moustache shone in their blackness. Ojebeta was moved. That she might once have married this handsome man! No, it could never have been possible. Clifford had been born into money and had acquired the ease of manner that only comfort and confidence could breed. She did not belong to that set of Ibos. She looked at her husband and saw a little untidy man, with his red eyes and his stubborn attitude to whatever he considered his, this fast ageing husband of hers who had to work so hard for their living in the Loco foundry workshop; and her heart went out to Jacob. Had she known how to demonstrate her feelings openly she would have extended her bony hand to touch that of her husband. She might belong to Jacob body and soul, but she loved it. She could think of no other suitable life for herself and for her ill-clad children. If Clifford was wearing that pitiable expression because he felt he should be sorry for her, he was mistaken. She was satisfied to belong to a man like Jacob, a fellow townsman, one who would never call her a slave, and who gave her a real home, even if it was only one room that served for sitting, eating, sleeping and everything else. She would rather have this than be a slave in a big house in Onitsha.

It never occurred to her that the big house could be sold or that, if she had married Clifford, she might have become a changed person with different values who would not have felt so alien in a luxurious house. What was the point of speculation?

"Welcome," she intoned. "This is my husband," she said gesturing towards the red-eyed Jacob. "And these are my brothers." Owezim and Okolie stood by uneasily.

Clifford was invited to sit on one of the straight-backed chairs ranged alongside the wall facing the curtained bed. Ojebeta enquired after everyone and Clifford brought her up to date: Jienuaka was now a successful businessman in Otu and had married Nwayinuzo; her friend Amanna had also gone into business and had a big shop, and a car, and though she was now widowed after her husband of only a few years had died, she was fine and happy. Chiago was living happily with Pa Palagada and their four growing sons.

"I send them to school because Father is too old to work now. To bring in more money I joined the army," Clifford added proudly.

There were other questions Ojebeta wanted to ask, about whether he himself had married, about the condition of the big house; but a sharp glance from Jacob sent her back to the kitchen to finish her cooking and leave the men to finalise the arrangements for her permanent ownership.

When Ojebeta had left the room her menfolk started to drink heavily, while making sure that Clifford drank more than any of them. After all, he was the guest, and besides they wanted to conclude the unsavoury business when he was in no mood to protest about any of their proposals that he give up all claims to Ojebeta. Jacob went behind the curtain and brought out an Ibo Bible.

"Now," he began, with a loud hiccough, "to pay back our debt of twenty-eight years ago. We have to thank you once more, but I hope you bear no malice against us."

"Malice?" hiccoughed Clifford. "Not at all. Ojebeta did not like me, so she married you and now I want my money back. The money my mother paid this man Okolie for her. All I want is my money and you can go to . . . I mean, you can go on being happy."

They all laughed. Then Jacob held the Bible like a talisman in front of Clifford. "Swear by this Bible that you will not wish my wife evil, not harm her or her children any more."

So saying, Jacob placed the Bible on a small table covered with one of the table cloths Ojebeta had crocheted in Otu Onitsha and kept for very special occasions such as this. "Swear by this, my friend. Swear!" He placed the eight pounds in single notes on the back of the Ibo Bible which had a gold cross embossed on it.

"I have never harmed your wife or your children," Clifford thought, but decided to say nothing. Maybe this was just as well. He was getting the money back, even though there had been no witness to the original transaction and promises. Okolie could very easily have denied it all, had he not been the type who would never dream of changing his word for fear of what the gods would do to him. Clifford could guess that although this was a religious family it practised a kind of Christianity that was heavily tinged with superstition. He was right; for as soon as he finished swearing that he would take the money gratefully and not have any bad motive against Ojebeta and her children, her elder brother Owezim, who was wearing a big colonial helmet inside the house, brought out some native chalk from inside his wide khaki shorts and made a circle on the cement floor. He broke a piece of kolanut, placed the pieces inside the circle and said:

"Now we have finished with the white man's God, you have to promise our dead parents that you have forgiven Ojebeta for marrying our good in-law Jacob here."

Clifford was by now amused and might have laughed out loud but for the fact that he noticed that the three men were very serious and that they really believed he still regretted not marrying this now nervous woman with lustreless air and disordered manners, not much better than the native women he saw by the wayside markets in Otu, too poor to own stalls. He could not help comparing her with Rosemary, the girl he was going to marry when he left the army. He was glad now that he had taken so long to make up his mind about any girl. Suppose he had submitted to his whims years ago and married Ojebeta, because his mother consented — what would have happened? He would surely have left her, or used her as a kitchen wife while marrying someone else for public presentation.

He swore his promises again, the native way. Then the money was recounted into his outstretched hand by Okolie, since it had been he who accepted it in the first instance.

Ojebeta came in then, carrying two bowls, one containing a heap of white, steaming rice, the other full of hot chicken stew. She was just in time to see Clifford stacking the eight pound notes into his leather Kano purse, and she knew what had happened and smiled gratefully at Jacob.

"The contract is completed, after all these years. I feel free in belonging to a new master from my very own town Ibuza; my mind is now at rest."

She placed the bowls of food on a small table that had been hastily pushed into the centre of the one-room apartment. Then she walked round to where Jacob was sitting feeling very important and expansive, and she knelt down in front of him.

"Thank you, my new owner. Now I am free in your house. I could not wish for a better master."

"Women," laughed Owezim, "they love to see money spent on them."

"Yes," agreed Clifford. "They love to know that they cost a lot of money."

Ojebeta giggled like a young girl of fifteen. For had she not been rightly valued? Would her mother Umeadi have wished another life for her daughter? Was the glory of a woman not a man, as the Ibuza people said?

So as Britain was emerging from war once more victorious, and claiming to have stopped the slavery which she had helped to spread in all her black colonies, Ojebeta, now a woman of thirty-five, was changing masters.